THE MOUSE MARATHON

The Mouse Marathon

OVIDIA YU

Marshall Cavendish Editions

© 2021 Ovidia Yu

First published in 1993 by Times Editions

This edition published in 2021 by Marshall Cavendish Editions
An imprint of Marshall Cavendish International

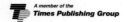

Other Marshall Cavendish Offices:
Marshall Cavendish Corporation, 800 Westchester Ave, Suite N-641, Rye Brook,
NY 10573, USA • Marshall Cavendish International (Thailand) Co Ltd, 253 Asoke,
16th Floor, Sukhumvit 21 Road, Klongtoey Nua, Wattana, Bangkok 10110, Thailand
• Marshall Cavendish (Malaysia) Sdn Bhd, Times Subang, Lot 46, Subang Hi-Tech
Industrial Park, Batu Tiga, 40000 Shah Alam, Selangor Darul Ehsan, Malaysia

Marshall Cavendish is a registered trademark of Times Publishing Limited

National Library Board, Singapore Cataloguing in Publication Data

Name(s): Yu, Ovidia, 1961-
Title: The mouse marathon / Ovidia Yu.
Other title(s): Marshall Cavendish classics.
Description: Singapore : Marshall Cavendish Editions, 2021. | First published in 1993
by Times Editions.
Identifier(s): OCN 1253279549 | ISBN 978-981-4974-54-7 (paperback)
Subject(s): LCSH: Interpersonal relations--Fiction. | Women employees--Fiction. |
Singapore--Fiction.
Classification: DDC S823--dc23

Printed in Singapore

Contents

The Mouse Marathon 7

Across the Causeway 14

Sociology 101 25

Well Now, My Love 28

The Start-Up Pick-Up 34

What The New Straits Times Said 38

Male Subjugation 39

Behind the News 49

Home Is Where the Heart Is 55

What The New Paper Said 62

Papaya Farms 63

Walkman and Woman 70

Poh Poh 83

There Will Always Be a Raffles 88

Mrs. White Had a Fright 97

At the Delphi 99

Fear of Flying 107

After Dinner 114

Strangers in the Night 119

Introducing the Late Ralph Lake 123

I Get No Kick From This Pain ... 127

A Sign 135

Leaving on a Jet Plane 137

Indonesia with Steve 139

When Will I See You Again? 143
Bandung 147
Final Connections 157
That's My Baby 162
Tangkuban Perahu 163
7:35 P.M. 169

The Mouse Marathon

Early Monday morning sunshine glinted off glass and metal fittings on Shenton Way skyscrapers rinsed to freshness by the previous night's rain.

Brightly coloured cars beetled swiftly along expressways as SBC's Radio One DJ reported *no* major traffic congestion along *any* of the major freeways. All the signs pointed to yet another beautiful and prosperous day in sunny, stable Singapore and possible new highs on the ST index; but as Lee Jaylin drove grimly in the direction of the Stead-Semple offices, she was less than full of eager anticipation of the day to come.

Lee Jaylin had spent the best part of the past weekend trying to psyche herself into her new project, but all her efforts seemed to have done her little good. No matter how hard she tried, Lee Jaylin simply could not throw herself body and soul into designer condoms.

Now, if a fresh young executive had come up to Jaylin with precisely the same dilemma, Jaylin would have said briskly, "You don't have to believe in it, you just have to sell it. Image Advertising is a business, not a religion!"

But now even that familiar old catechism failed to comfort her.

What is Image Advertising all about, anyway?

Creating an ideal lifestyle.

Creating lust for that ideal lifestyle.

Mesmerization of the masses.

But how could you think about mesmerizing the masses when you couldn't even convince yourself that what you were doing was worth doing?

It wasn't just a matter of the designer condom. Considered as a thing in itself, the designer condom was an acceptable concept, an admirable concept, even. Jaylin's sharp market instincts told her that once their client's condom was launched, all the other major design houses would be kicking themselves for not having come up with the idea first. Once the designer condom became a status symbol, Safe Sex would really take off – as the best way to show off *all* your assets.

And yet, at the brink of this breakthrough, Lee Jaylin found herself wondering, *why am I doing this?* interspersed with, *how much longer can I go on doing this?* and even, *what will all this be worth in twenty, thirty, a hundred years' time?*

This was all Gerry's fault, of course.

But Jaylin had resolved not to think about Geraldine Lai and the fact that that irresponsible woman was leaving for America that very day.

Unlike *some* people, Lee Jaylin was a responsible career woman with a full day ahead of her.

Jaylin's faithful personal assistant, Mun Ee, was already in the office when Jaylin got in. She always was. Mun Ee knew better than anyone else where Jaylin's records were filed, when Jaylin would be free to lunch, which calls should be relayed through, and how to keep Jaylin functioning smoothly. Minutes after Jaylin's elevator reached her 14th floor office, Mun Ee whipped a freshly brewed mug of scalding black coffee on to Jaylin's desk and hovered with updates to the day's schedule as Jaylin sipped.

"Raffles Multiplex called to cancel this morning's meeting," Mun Ee said.

"Why?"

"Maria Fernandez Gong can't make it. She said it was 'urgent personal business' and she would explain it to you herself when you came in."

Gerry hadn't liked Maria, Jaylin thought.

Why are you thinking of Gerry's dislike in the past tense? Gerry's shown no sign of changing her mind about Maria Fernandez Gong.

Or was it Gerry herself that she was thinking of in the past tense?

Stop right there. Don't waste time. Focus on Raffles Multiplex. Come on.

Jaylin had fought hard for Stead-Semple to accept the Raffles Multiplex account after Maria Gong approached her personally.

Jaylin' s Senior Partner had been openly sceptical: "Raffles Multiplex has already fired two agencies in three years. It's a disaster area. They don't know what they want and then they blame you for everything that goes wrong including the weather. There's a jinx on that project. I'm not keen on adding Stead-Semple to their list of victims."

Jaylin had taken the professional approach. She appealed to his wife.

"If we pull this off, it will be a real coup … "

"Oh, go ahead if you want to," Linda Caisely-Stead said. "But *charge* those buggers."

All those months ago, Jaylin had been dead certain that

the Raffles Multiplex account was one worth cultivating. Now she was beginning to wonder if she had made a mistake. Her doubts focused mainly on their client's representative, Mrs. Maria Fernandez Gong, and could not be entirely blamed on Jaylin's current career malaise.

Long, long ago, in a social milieu far, far away, Lee Jaylin and Maria Fernandez had been neighbouring hostelites and fellow students at the National University of Singapore. Later still, they split the rent for a UDMC house in Normanton Estate for a couple of years as they set themselves up in their respective careers.

The passing years had left them little in common. Maria married and produced one, then two, then three children in quick succession and moved into a different sphere altogether.

She had even taken on a different *look*.

The warm, fun-loving girl with an infectious laugh had matured into a defensive, chain-smoking woman with a dis-contented air; and the tantalizing 'come hither' in her eyes had withered into a querulous 'where have you been?'

Though four months younger than Jaylin, Maria looked at least 10 years older. The passing years had dealt very differently with them … or perhaps it was they who had dealt differently with the passing years? To be honest, Jaylin was surprised to find Maria Gong handling the account for Raffles Multiplex.

Jaylin was finding doing business with Maria exhausting because Maria was always full of non-business complaints about her boss and his unreasonable demands, her husband and his irresponsible debts, her children and their problems in school … and it could be difficult steering her back on track.

Remembering that years ago, she herself had warned Maria against the haste with which she plunged into maternity and matrimony, dragging her vaguely aimless boyfriend after her, Jaylin thought the least Maria could do now was spare her the dreary details.

Though verbally sympathetic, Jaylin couldn't understand why a woman, if such misery was genuine, didn't kill herself and end it once and for all.

Had Maria cancelled the meeting because she was busy gassing herself and her three children in the kitchen of her flat in Braddell Heights?

"Jaylin? Jaylin, are you all right?" Mun Ee's worried voice broke into Jaylin's thoughts.

"Yes, the designer condom is a good idea," Jaylin said vaguely.

Mun Ee looked reassured. As long as the Boss was focused on work, all was right with the world. Of course, it was not Mun Ee's place to tell that all was not well with the Boss.

"I'll come back later," Mun Ee made a graceful exit.

With Mun Ee gone, Jaylin took her first Pepsi of the day out of the mini-fridge against the wall behind her table. The caffeine in the Pepsi-Cola charged up her metabolism to a level where she burnt off the extra sugar it added to her blood stream. Jaylin actually lost weight if she drank too much Pepsi. But those cans of Pepsi-Cola were an indispensable part of her office routine. Jaylin could slide her chair back, open the fridge, pick out a can, ease up the tab and slide back up to her desk all without letting go of the phone for a moment.

"You're addicted to the stuff," Gerry used to tell her. "You're addicted to your Pepsi and your work. Why do you have to be so obsessive about everything? You're sick and you won't admit it! Why do you push so hard for jobs you're not even keen on handling? Why take them on in the first place? There's more to life than working 16-hour days, you know!"

Well, what else was there in her life?

Jaylin enjoyed her work. She enjoyed the adrenalin rush that it brought her. She liked the way clients and projects threw up stress and problems that focused her attention on finding alternatives, finding solutions ... clear-cut solutions.

Even as a schoolgirl, Jaylin had preferred analytical problem-solving to more creative work. She had always enjoyed the challenge of arriving at the right answer. But what if you were to discover, after years of right answers, that you had been answering all the wrong questions?

Jaylin took a long swig of icy, effervescent Pepsi.

It was true what they said in the business; if you don't have time to think, you don't have time to have a breakdown.

So stop thinking. Get back to work. Designer condoms. Raffles Multiplex ...

And then there was Gerry, who had opted out. Geraldine Lai, who said she was sure there had to be more to life than this endless rat race ...

"We've only got one chance at life. I mean to get all I can out of it!" Gerry had said.

And Gerry had also said, "Come with me."

But Jaylin's work meant too much to her. To her it breathed life, stimulation, a reason for getting up in the mornings, her raison d'etre ... the only way she had of proving to herself that she was a worthwhile person.

"Please think about it. Take a year off. You know you can afford it."

But Jaylin had had too many commitments, too many projects pending ...

So Gerry had taken off alone.

And Jaylin was left with designer condoms and Raffles Multiplex on her mind. She was feeling weary, and also feeling, for the first time, that she was not so much a part of the rat race as a long and lonely mouse marathon.

Across the Causeway

Across the Causeway, Ralph Emerson Lake checked into the Kuala Lumpur Executive Spa.

"Well hey, look who's back again!" he said loudly and jovially to the pretty receptionist. "Did you miss me, Sweetie? Couldn't stay away from you for long, could I? Anything interesting happen around here while I was gone?"

"Siapa itu?" the less-pretty receptionist asked the pretty receptionist when the *mat salleh* had gone up to his room.

"Tak tau. Kurang ajak!"

Up in his room Ralph Lake ordered breakfast and an English language newspaper before showering. Then he spread the paper on the bed and read it while he breakfasted in the nude.

"Impossible!" he said aloud. "Ridiculous! Pathetic!"

To the average, unjaded eye, there was nothing particularly impossible, ridiculous or pathetic in the day's reporting, but Ralph believed that being appalled (with an American accent) by the standard of newspaper reportage in Malaysia and Singapore gave him an air of cosmopolitan sophistication.

And Ralph Lake had to practice his air of cosmopolitan sophistication. Ralph Lake had to prepare himself for what he had come to Kuala Lumpur to do.

Once breakfast was out of the way, Ralph picked up the phone and dialled a local number – a bungalow in Damansara

Heights. He was pleased when the phone was answered with a faint Filipino accent. He was a man who set great store by setting the scenario for the impression he made on people. It should be easy enough for him to impress a Filipina maid.

"Is my wife there?"

"Who's calling, please?"

"Never mind who's calling."

The woman didn't even have the courtesy to address him as 'sir'.

"Just let me speak to my wife!"

The woman remained confused, "Your wife? I think you have the wrong – "

These people probably hadn't even told the stupid girl that he was married to the daughter of the house.

"Please *listen* to me. Don't you understand simple English? I want to speak to Stephanie Lake … you may know her as Stephanie Chen."

"Stephanie Chen?" said the woman with a touch of hauteur. "Hold on a moment, please."

Ralph wondered why it was so impossible to teach these third-world peasants simple telephone manners. But who was to teach them? The Chinese? The Chinese were just as bad themselves.

But although he was comfortable in the consciousness of his American superiority in matters of telephone etiquette, Ralph's mouth was dry as he waited for his wife to come to the telephone.

It was more than a month since they had last spoken. It was more than six months since they had last met.

"Hello?" came his wife's warm, throaty voice.

"Hi there!" Ralph said effusively. "How's my girl?"

"Hello, who *is* this?" his girl said with suspicious wariness.

Hurt silence.

"Hello, hello?"

Most days, since moving out of her marital apartment in Pantai Hills and back into her parents' palatial Petaling Jaya bungalow, Stephanie Lake, *nee* Chen, managed not to think very much about her marital affairs.

After all, her marriage had only lasted six months. Stephanie was thirty-four years old now and six months was a very small fraction of her life, especially now that she had consigned it well into her past.

Because she thought about it so little, she couldn't say for certain just what had gone wrong with her marriage.

It may have been Ralph's frequent trips out of Malaysia, or it may have been realising that when Ralph returned from Singapore with one new condom it meant that he had used the other two in the packet with somebody else … or it may have been that Stephanie was tired – tired of thin, white hairy legs and that paunchy white belly and the unendearing way Ralph had of laughing shrilly at his own jokes. Whatever the reason, Stephanie woke up one morning knowing that she didn't want to be Mrs. Ralph Lake any more.

Ralph was on one of his flying visits to the States at the time, so Stephanie packed up her things, put a stack of Ralph's pornographic magazines down the garbage chute, and drove back to her parents' home.

Then Stephanie (through her lawyers) informed Ralph that she was putting their marital abode (the apartment, paid for by her parents, was in her name) up for sale. If Ralph wanted to buy it, he was welcome to make her an offer (via her lawyers).

Ralph pronounced himself totally at sea.

Stephanie didn't accuse him of anything so he genuinely had no idea which of his indiscretions had proved to be the last straw.

Ralph Lake was more embarrassed than anything else by his wife's desertion. He had told his friends in the States how his beautiful, docile and feminine third wife never complained about anything he did.

"Third time lucky you know, guys!"

And he had hinted to his friends back home that Asian women just oozed out of their panties at the thought of sex with a white American man ... How could he tell them, now, that his beautiful, docile, adoring third wife had just upped and walked out on him for no reason that he could see?

Ralph wasn't the only one who didn't understand why Stephanie had left him. Stephanie herself had never faced this question honestly. All her life, Stephanie had drifted into and out of situations as she pleased. Not justifying one's actions has always been the prerogative of wealthy non-politicians.

When the telephone rang in her home that morning, Ralph Lake had been the furthest thing from Stephanie's mind. She had been in the process of helping Rebecca A. plan her next exhibition. Over the past year or so, Stephanie had discovered in herself an hitherto unsuspected flair for designing and coordinating gallery shows. She had an eye for colour and decorating, and a genuine love for the work of local contemporary folk artists that made it possible for her to select and show them at their best. What had started out as a favour to a friend and a hobby to keep her mind off her marital breakdown had rapidly become a much sought-after service.

Rebecca A. had been expecting a long-distance call from *her* husband in Manila, which was why she had answered the phone when it rang.

"I'll give you a clue, Baby Doll," Ralph Lake said.

And Ralph Lake sang into the phone:

Darlin' Steffi, you're so fine
You get me drunk more quick than wine
Darlin' Steffi, I'm cuddlin' up to you …
Do-be-do-be-dooooo

Stephanie had always believed that one of the most romantic things that could happen to her, or to anyone else, was to have someone make up lyrics to a song just for her.

However, Ralph Lake had spoilt that notion for her once and for all, once he started composing lewd songs to her as part of his foreplay. He hadn't done it to upset her – in fact it almost wouldn't have been so bad if he *had* done it deliberately to upset her. The really sad thing was, Ralph Lake sang to Stephanie to try to *please* her. It was just one more thing that brought home to her how little she had in common with the man she'd married.

Even while they were still 'happily' married, Ralph Lake could spoil things for Stephanie without even *trying*. And now Ralph Lake was singing his own song to Stephanie over the telephone because he wanted to be cute and amusing.

"Ralph," Stephanie said weakly, more to stop him singing than anything else, "what a surprise!"

"How are you, Sweetie?" asked Ralph Lake in the husky,

would-be manly-affectionate, would-be sexy voice of a paunchy, balding, Caucasian man.

"Sweetie, I'm in KL on a flying visit – just stopping over, you know – "

"Oh?"

"So how are you, Pussycat?"

"Ralph, I've got somebody with me right now – "

"Aw come on. You can take a minute to tell me how you are! I worry about you, you know. No matter where I am, I think of you and wonder how you are."

"Ralph, the thing is, she's expecting a call. We've got somebody calling in to confirm some dates for bookings … "

"Not a good time, huh."

"No, it's not."

"I'd like to see you, Steffi."

"I'm very busy right now, Ralph. Maybe next time."

"I could drop by your place. Just to say 'hello' to your folks … "

"No, Ralph. Not a good idea."

"Not such a good idea, huh."

"No."

"So why don't you come on up to see me here? I've got a room at the Executive Spa. We can have a bit of privacy here."

"I don't know – "

"Come on, Sugarcakes, I just want to see you. You can give me 10 minutes of your time. Come on over and we'll have a drink or something. Or lunch. For Chrissakes, Stephanie, I just want to talk!"

"I've really got a hundred-and-one things to do today," Stephanie said.

Ralph put on his hurt, reasonable voice: "Look, Hon, I'm only in town for the day. Look, I just want to see you, talk to you, spend some time with you. We're supposed to be married. Is one lunch too much to ask?"

Stephanie hated it when Ralph put on his hurt, reasonable voice.

"This is not just a social call, Stephanie," said Ralph, "there's something very serious I need to discuss with you. Something very serious that concerns both of us."

"What is it?"

"We'll talk about it when you get here. The Executive Spa, room 710. Please be reasonable, Stephanie."

And Ralph Lake put down the telephone.

Stephanie jumped to the conclusion that Ralph wanted to talk to her about getting a divorce. She assumed that he had met the woman he wanted to make his fourth wife.

Stephanie wasn't very interested in the ins and outs of her husband's sex life. She knew that her husband had mistresses ("The only one who matters to me at all is you, Steffi. But a man has needs, and ... you know what I mean ... "). He had assured her that being paranoid about catching AIDS, he always used condoms. Once every few months, he went for an HIV test and took Stephanie out to celebrate when he was given a clean bill of health.

"It would be so ironic," he told her once.

"Why?" asked Stephanie.

"Because ... you know, because with me it's always been women, women, women ... "

"Men can get it from women too, can't they?"

"Yes, Sweetie. But I don't do drugs, I don't sleep with

men – that's what I mean. It would be so ironic … "

If anyone who slept around as much as Ralph Lake caught a Sexually Transmitted Disease, Stephanie wouldn't have called it ironic whether it was men or women he was sleeping with.

After Ralph's phone call, Stephanie found it difficult to bring her mind back to the gallery layout and their lighting plans.

"Oh, go and meet him," Rebecca A. told her. "Meet him and get it over with. The thing you dread is always more terrible than the thing you face."

"I suppose," said Stephanie vaguely.

"Men," said Rebecca A., "they are all the same."

"I hope not," said Stephanie, who tended to be optimistic by nature.

After Rebecca A. left, Stephanie surprised herself by dressing up as though she was getting ready for a big date.

She washed her hair.

She revarnished her nails.

Then she confronted the problem of what she was going to wear. In front of the mirror, Stephanie tried to decide between a very nice dusky pink-fitted silk crepe dress with a low draped collar … so sexy, but so demure … or a matronly classic print *Diane Freis* …

Her Aunt Charlotte came into her bedroom without knocking.

"Can you give me a lift into town?"

"Ummm. Where to?"

"Where are you going?"

"The Executive Spa."

"Why?"

"Business."

"You're going to meet That Man, aren't you?"

Sometimes Charlotte could be unnervingly astute. Either she was psychic or she listened in on other people's phone conversations.

"Well, actually, yes."

"I don't think you should meet him. I don't think you should meet him alone."

"Aunty Charlotte, we're just going to have lunch. He's got something he wants to discuss with me."

'I'm coming with you."

"No, Aunty Charlotte, there's no need."

"I don't like that man."

"I happen to be married to 'that man', remember? He wants to talk to me, that's all. I'm going to talk to him, that's all."

"Are you two going to get a divorce or what?"

"I don't know. Maybe. I suppose, eventually. Yes."

"I don't suppose there's any chance of you sorting things out and getting back together?"

It was typical of Stephanie's Aunt Charlotte to warn her against meeting Ralph and then urge her, without any change in tone, to get back together with him for the rest of her life . . .

"No, Aunty Charlotte. No way."

"Don't use that tone with me. I don't think you should wear the pink. You don't want to look as though you're trying to entice him back."

"Hmmm," said Stephanie, her eyes fixed on the mirror.

"Stephanie," said her aunt, "just let me say this one

thing once and I won't mention it again. We have never had a divorce in our family. Just remember that."

Aunt Charlotte had already mentioned that 'one thing once' to Stephanie several times in the recent past.

Stephanie was well aware that they had never had a divorce in their family. She just didn't know what her aunt expected her to do with this information.

Stephanie's parents had been in England when Stephanie was born, and Stephanie's Aunt Charlotte had gone over to help Stephanie's mother with the baby. Ever since then, she had lived with the family and fussed over Stephanie more than Stephanie's own mother did.

Stephanie knew that her intentions were good, but she could still be a bit of a nuisance ...

Stephanie settled on a magnolia silk velvet tunic with a sashed front over raspberry velour leggings. This was her *Thomas Wee* confident-beauty-in-unpleasant-situations ensemble. She had discovered it down in Singapore and to her it symbolized all the breezy brashness of that island's women.

When Stephanie found herself in her *Thomas Wee,* she realised that this was the day she was going to do something about her marriage once and for all.

She didn't know *what* it was that she was going to do yet, but she hoped that something would occur to her when the time was right ...

Forty-five minutes later, Stephanie stood outside Ralph Lake's room on the seventh floor of The Kuala Lumpur Executive Spa. It occurred to her that she could either ring the door bell or turn around and buy a plane ticket for Maui and disappear forever with a new identity.

The thought of packing for Maui at such short notice was a daunting one.

Stephanie rang the door bell.

Sociology 101

Sociology lecturer Dr. Lim SuFern heaved her burden of paper on to the desk in her office with a small sigh of relief. While it was debatable whether or not first year National University of Singapore sociology students were getting better at solving sociological problems, they were certainly handing in more paper. Lecturers were developing biceps and joking about their marking *load*.

Lim SuFern looked out of the misted-over window panes at the carefully landscaped portion of Kent Ridge visible from her office. Now that she was over fifty, the weather brought on a dull ache in her left leg that might be the beginning of rheumatism, but she liked the heavy rain, the moist, cool air and the fresh smell of damp earth.

Even after so many years, the steady wet drumming, the air-conditioned chill and the vapour that condensed against the cold glass still reminded her of her student days in London. In those days, an independent life as a career academic had only been a dream she barely dared to articulate.

SuFern had gone to England by ship, a journey that had taken over a month. By ocean liner! Today the idea suggests luxury cruises for the idle classes, but in those days it had simply been the only practical way to travel. She had been so seasick just before they docked at Bombay; seasick, scared and already homesick for the mother and sisters she was leaving for the first time. But, in Bombay, SuFern took her first step on foreign soil and everything became miraculously all right. She had never forgotten the heady, dizzying excitement, *I'm really here, I'm really here, I'm really here,* standing on the hot, noisy, smelly dock and realising for the first time that her destiny was in her hands and the whole world lay open before her.

Already, SuFern was beginning to forget little things that happened last month, last year. Absent-mindedness, she told herself. She joked with her colleagues. *I want to save what memory cells I have left for really important things!*

But she knew that she would remember that day, that moment, that instant of revelation in Bombay for the rest of her life. She had never gone back to Bombay again, nor had she wanted to. She did not want to betray the memory.

The most frightening thing about time passing was not how long ago it had been that one young girl became aware of her selfhood and thrilled to feel a world opening up before her ... but that that moment could seem like it was only yesterday to a fifty-five-year-old woman who at times still felt like that young girl. The world had changed beyond anything she could have imagined then; where had that kampong reared child-woman on her way to university in London gone?

SuFern pulled her attention away from the rain spattered window and sat down at her desk. Reminiscences could wait. She could sit and reminisce all day long after her sight and hearing failed her. But for now, the sooner she got this last batch of papers marked and graded, the sooner she could get down to some *real* work of her own. She put on her reading glasses and picked up her pen.

But though she bent industriously to her marking, her mind kept wandering back to its current pet obsession – *Male Subjugation* ...

Well Now, My Love

"Well now, my love," Stephanie's husband laid out his business proposition before her.

"You see," said Ralph Lake, earnestly and convincingly, "we have to get a hold of five hundred thousand Sing dollars right away."

"Right away," Stephanie repeated vaguely, hearing but not really listening to him.

Stephanie was thinking about Ralph's use of the word 'we'. Ralph said 'we' so easily, but it was a long time since Stephanie had thought of the two of them as a unit that could be classified as 'we' in any practical sense of the word. She was also wondering whether it was Ralph who was particularly unpredictable or whether it was she who was particularly bad at predicting what he was going to come up with next.

Until she arrived in his hotel room, Stephanie had been so certain they were finally going to sit down and discuss their dead marriage and the steps needed to legalize its demise. She had thought up some tactful phrases to ease the situation along should their meeting face to face feel awkward.

It all happened so suddenly. I think we got married before we had a chance to get to know each other ... there doesn't have to be a villain here, Ralph. We can part as friends ...

Stephanie had also decided that she wasn't going to bring up his suspected infidelities or the fact that her family (i.e.

Aunt Charlotte) had never liked him – unless he pushed her into a corner.

But instead, Ralph had launched into a sales spiel, a business proposition. Stephanie realised, all over again, just how little she knew this man she had married.

Ralph was irritated by the absent look on his beautiful wife's face. It hadn't been easy for him to decide to come all the way to KL and talk to her. The least she could do was pay attention to what he had to say for 10 minutes.

"Do you understand me, Steffi Honey?" he asked her with exaggerated patience.

Stephanie looked at him with an unreadable expression on her lovely face. Her eyes were blank beneath those incredible lashes. She was so beautiful. If only she would pull herself together a little, Ralph thought, she could have been such an asset to him.

But no, she preferred to fritter her life away.

"How soon do you need all this money?" Stephanie wanted to know.

"Within a week. Let's say, by Friday."

"Ralph, you know I don't have that kind of cash."

"I know you don't," Ralph said even more patiently.

"You'll have to speak to your father."

"No."

Stephanie gave Ralph a look that said that was her final word on the subject.

"No?"

Ralph gave Stephanie a look that said he was terribly disappointed in her lack of trust in him.

"Stephanie Sweetie, let's be reasonable. Look, there's no risk involved, it's only a loan … "

"No, Ralph."

"I just need to have the money in the bank on Monday. On Tuesday, once the deal is signed, you'll get every cent back, I swear!"

"No, Ralph. No."

The corners of Ralph's mouth straightened and turned down. He threw up his hands in a what-can-I-say-to-such-a-moron gesture and sighed over the stupidity and short-sightedness of young Malaysian heiresses.

Stephanie decided that it was time for her to leave. She stood up.

"Do you need money for the hotel here? I could – "

Ralph turned and launched a new attack on a new front: "Damn it, Stephanie. I'm not talking about peanuts, I'm not talking about *hotel bills.* I'm talking about making more money than you can *imagine* and you don't want to have anything to do with it. I don't understand you – look, I'm not having a problem with money here – "

Ralph picked up the telephone. "Room Service? This is room 710. I want two bottles of champagne in my room. The best that you've got. Yes, now. Immediately. Thank you. You have a nice day, too."

"You see? Around here, they know how to treat a man with some respect. They know how to recognise *potential* when they see it. They – "

Ralph lifted his hands and shook his head as though his exasperation rendered him speechless.

"Then why don't you ask *them* for the money?" Stephanie said reasonably.

Ralph looked at her for a long moment. She looked right back at him.

"You've changed, Stephanie. You changed when I let you talk to Antonia. I should never have let you talk to Antonia. I told you that Karen never liked Antonia!"

Antonia Garcia had been Ralph's second wife. Ralph had introduced Stephanie to Antonia when they visited New York on their honeymoon. Antonia had said to Stephanie, "Good old Ralphie just had to show me he's got himself a better wife than I was to him. But I hope we can be friends. Women have more important things to do with their lives than fight over men!"

Stephanie had been intimidated by Antonia, but she had liked her.

Karen Auer had been Ralph's first wife. She lived in Seattle, but Ralph had telephoned her from New York and handed the receiver over for Stephanie to say 'Hello'.

All that Karen said to Stephanie was, "Good luck to you. You don't know how much I mean that!"

Stephanie had thought that that was nice of Karen, but Ralph said Karen was just being snide.

"You think I'm going to take off with your father's money, right? You think that, don't you? I can tell that that's what you're thinking. I'm glad I've found out what you think of me, Stephanie. Why ever did you marry me, Stephanie? Have you ever wondered? Why did you marry me if you don't even trust me? I ask myself that and I just don't have an answer!"

At last Ralph and Stephanie were on the same wavelength. Stephanie didn't have an answer to that question either.

Ralph walked out on to the balcony and stood there looking down with his back to Stephanie.

His back expressed injured dignity.

Stephanie decided that this was an appropriate moment to slip away. Ralph didn't seem to be in the right frame of mind to discuss a divorce.

"Stephanie," Ralph said quietly.

Stephanie turned with the door already open in her hand. Ralph was carefully rising into a standing position on top of the balcony wall ...

"I think you should know that you've just cost me my entire career, my entire reputation, my entire credibility in the business, in the region – "

"Ralph! No!" cried Stephanie, flabbergasted.

"You've left me with no choice, Stephanie!"

"Ralph, stop it! Look, I'll get you the money somehow! Get down from there! Please, Ralph!"

Ralph's face creased into a smile. He crowed, "I knew you'd see sense, Steffi Baby! I knew you still cared about me – "

Then the door opened wider against Stephanie's hand and a trolley bumped its way in.

"Room Service," said the girl who was pushing it in. She picked up the tray with its two bottles of *Dom Perignon* and four champagne glasses and waited for Stephanie to indicate where she wanted it.

Then the girl saw Ralph standing on the ledge.

The tray fell, the waitress screamed, two bottles of *Dom Perignon* and four champagne glasses smashed ...

Startled, Stephanie jumped.

So did Ralph.

Seven floors.
Or would you say he fell?

Stephanie froze motionless where she stood, her hand still clamped to the door knob.

"I killed him," she whispered, "I killed him, I killed him, I killed him ... "

Then she vomited all over her *Thomas Wee*.

The Start-Up Pick-Up

Dead.

On the long and winding road that should have led to her door. South Buona Vista Road, to be precise. Lee Jaylin's little black European car had just died on her *again*. Every time this happened, Jaylin swore she was going to junk the temperamental European vehicle and buy herself a stolid, reliable, economic Japanese car. But still, when it was running, it ran like a dream …

She had always felt a certain sentimental loyalty to the make and she didn't want to drive a BM or a Merc like everyone else, but enough was enough. This time, for sure, she was going to trade it in for a Subaru.

Jaylin pulled up the handbrake and tried to remember where the nearest bus-stop/call phone was. Would it be more practical to start walking (in the rain) in the direction of the hospital, or (just as much in the rain) in the direction of the famous duck rice shops at the Pasir Panjang Road junction? A long and wearing day that had not begun well and had not got better had just hit its nadir.

Cars pulled up behind hers and cautiously edged around, their lights shining yellow in the drizzly dusk. People looked through their rain-streaked windows with a mixture of impatience and sympathy.

More sympathy than impatience, because Jaylin was a woman.

A taxi negotiated around her stationary vehicle. Jaylin made a half-hearted attempt to flag it down, to no avail. The rain seemed to be coming down even more heavily than before. It was February ... were they still in the monsoon season?

Now that most of her waking hours were spent enclosed in air-conditioned de-humidified spaces, Jaylin had completely lost track of the seasons.

It was becoming damp and stuffy inside the car and the rain was getting in through the crack of window she had left open in a feeble attempt at ventilation.

Jaylin did not take well to forced inactivity. She made a decision and slipped the catch on her seat belt. If she got out and walked, the worst that could happen was that she would get wet.

She got out of her car, trying to manoeuvre her umbrella, her keys, her shoulder bag and her briefcase with some semblance of dignity. She would walk for it, as far as the nearest public phone. Once there she would call her mechanic and give him hell.

Right then, Jaylin would have sold her soul for a cold Pepsi. She would have sold her soul for a *warm* Pepsi.

Then a dark green Volvo purred to a stop in front of her car and a middle-aged woman with short, greying hair wound down the driver's window to say, "Hello! Are you having a problem?"

Wasn't it obvious?

"Kind of. Yes."

"Are you out of petrol?"

"No."

"Tell you what," said the woman – she had an air of sensible authority, "put on your hazards, lock your car and leave it. I'll give you a ride to somewhere *dry* with a telephone."

"I would really appreciate it, if it's not too much trouble … "

"Of course not!" said the woman warmly. "Just put your things on the back seat and get in yourself … "

So this was how Jaylin found herself inside a strange dark green Volvo driven by a strange woman.

Perhaps she would get herself a nice, reliable Volvo.

"I really appreciate your stopping. I'm sorry I'm getting your seat all wet."

"No problem. Don't worry. It will dry. I think it's supposed to be waterproof. Do you live near here?"

"Very, actually. On Pasir Panjang Road. Just beyond Haw Par Villa."

"Oh, in that case, I'll run you home – no, that's all right. It's the logical solution. You want to get out of those wet clothes before you catch cold."

"Thanks so much. Wow, this is another one up for the female species!"

The woman gave Jaylin a strange look. Jaylin laughed apologetically, "Well, I mean, look at all those male drivers who could have stopped and didn't … no, don't listen to me. People are always accusing me of male bashing. Do you work or live around here?"

"Work, actually. At NUS. I was just on my way home … look, I'll just give you my card – " the woman reached across Jaylin to flip open the glove compartment and hand her a card case.

Jaylin took a card out and put the elegant ebony case back in the glove compartment. The name on the card rang a distant bell, but she couldn't place it immediately.

"You're a senior lecturer at NUS?"

"Yes. Would you like to get together for a drink some time? I'd like to talk to you … "

Jaylin studied the name card, then glanced at the woman in the driver's seat. Dr. Lim SuFern, Senior Lecturer with the Sociology Department of NUS, didn't *look* much like a woman who would stop for the victim of a stalled car on the off-chance of a quick pick-up.

Which was a pity.

Jaylin liked this mature, quietly efficient woman with her briskly unabashed actions. *Why was her name so familiar?*

"I'd like that. I'd like that very much," she said.

"Well good," said Dr. Lim. "What's a convenient time? What about tonight?"

Jaylin sneezed. And again. She always sneezed when she was nervous.

"Should I turn down the air-conditioning?" Dr. Lim asked, concerned.

"No, it's fine, thank you."

What about tonight? It's Monday night, after all. We can always celebrate surviving Monday …

"Tonight?"

"Unless you have other plans for dinner?"

"Excuse me, Dr. Lim. You'll have to slow down … "

"I beg your pardon?"

"It's the next house on the right."

What The New Straits Times Said

An American tourist fell to his death from the balcony of his room in Kuala Lumpur's Executive Spa yesterday.

The death of Ralph Emerson Lake, 39, was witnessed by his wife Madam Chen Lay Hoon, 34, and a waitress, Salimah Salim, who are currently helping the Police with their investigations.

Male Subjugation

"Dr. Lim SuFern! Oh, oh, what an unexpected pleasure!" Jaylin's grandmother did not need to be introduced to Jaylin's rescuer.

"I've attended all your public lectures, Dr. Lim! And I've always been meaning to tell you how much I enjoy your work!"

And the name Dr. Lim SuFern was not unfamiliar to her step-grandfather either.

"This is my grandfather, Robert Celli ... "

"Dr. Lim, it's good to meet you at last. I've been hearing a lot about your work. My wife is a great fan of yours. She's always trying to keep me in line with theories that she picks up at your talks!"

'Tm sorry, Mr. Celli! I hope that hasn't made life too painful for you!"

"Not at all, Dr. Lim, not at all."

"What are you going on about, Robert? Please take a seat, Dr. Lim. Make yourself comfortable. Can I get you something to drink? Will you stay to dinner?"

"I'll just go and change into something dry," Jaylin said, amused and a little bemused by SuFern's reception. Even her grandmother's small brown and white cat seemed excited, rubbing herself against SuFern's ankles with little squeaks of welcome.

"I won't be long."

As she walked down the corridor to her bedroom, Jaylin could hear her grandmother saying earnestly, "And what are you working on at the moment, Dr. Lim, anything interesting?"

Jaylin had not anticipated this. Her grandparents were politely mild senior citizens who were usually ensconced in their own, politely mild concerns. But Lim SuFern looked well accustomed to handling such situations.

"Do call me SuFern, Mrs. Celli," came SuFern's clear, calm voice from the living room.

Dr. Lim SuFern *sounded* well capable of handling the situation.

"I'm so sorry," Jaylin told SuFern later, as she ran her eyes down the menu. She was back in dry clothes, seated in a familiar hotel coffee house, and trying to fit back into her own persona.

"I knew your name sounded familiar – I just couldn't place you right away, with the car and the rain and everything … I've read about you, of course. And my grandmother's mentioned you … it's just that for some reason, I assumed you would be much, much older."

'I'm probably much, much older than you think I am!" SuFern smiled. "But I'm comfortable with my age, so please don't feel you have to tell me how little I look it!"

Indeed, SuFern did seem comfortable with her age, much more so than Jaylin, who at the moment was feeling old and worn out and run down. She had wanted to get out of the house and away from her grandmother's excited chatter, but now she felt uncharacteristically near to tears.

In fact, Jaylin felt as though she was just getting over a particularly bad bout of flu – trembly and dejected and weak as a kitten – which would have been fine if she *had* been getting over the flu, only she wasn't. Physically, she was fine. Workwise she had nothing to complain about. What, then, was wrong with her?

Lim SuFern was a relative stranger, but Jaylin felt a strong compulsion to lay her problems before this woman. At the same time, she felt the equal and opposite compulsion to create the impression of a reserved but incredibly successful advertising executive.

Jaylin studied her menu with more attention than it really merited. She couldn't seem to reach a decision there either.

Lim SuFern's menu was already closed on the table. SuFern sat facing Jaylin with her fingers interlaced over her menu, waiting patiently.

"You're the feminist theorist who says that feminists should ease up on male bashing," Jaylin said, for the sake of saying something halfway intelligent. "Is that what you wanted to talk to me about?"

"I think that everybody has been doing too much 'bash-ing'," SuFern said. "Actually, my field is psychosociology. I was interested in a phrase you used earlier in my car. You said 'one up for the female species' as though you were keeping score for 'your' side. I thought that was very interesting. I highly recommend the grilled sea-bass, by the way. It's a healthier choice."

Jaylin folded her menu shut. The management executive in her wasn't sure it liked being taken in hand so quickly and completely. On the other hand, the child in her relished the motherly tone. Would an academic psychosociologist put this down to the very un-motherly nature of her own mother?

"Two grilled sea-bass," SuFern said to their waiter with a smile. Jaylin wondered whether the waiter thought she was out with her mother. Except that Dr. Lim SuFern wasn't *anything* like Jaylin's mother.

"Let me tell you a little about the subject I'm working on now – Male Subjugation."

Male Subjugation?

As she spoke, SuFern was pulling a scribble book out of the file carrier that apparently served her as a handbag.

"These are some of the things that women say about men. Listen to this: 'I believe that women have a capacity for understanding and compassion that a man structurally does not have, does not have because he cannot have it. He's just incapable of it.'

"Now, this is not just any woman speaking, this is Barbara Jordan, ethics advisor to the Governor of Texas. Then there's Houston mayor Kathy Whitmire who's on record saying that men are less intelligent than women. These women are political chauvinists. If they had been talking about any other group of people – women, Hispanics, homosexuals, left-handed teachers – they would be run out of public life, but men are too cowed to defend themselves. Yes, I realise that I'm using American examples, but everybody all over the world is jumping on the bandwagon. I even saw a magazine article that claims women bond better with pet rabbits than a man ever could … "

"Maybe it's true," said Jaylin, "I don't mean about men being less intelligent, but the part about men not bonding with bunnies might be true. But does it really matter? And I don't think anybody here really believes that men are less

42

intelligent – maybe they're just less sensitive, less considerate, less tactful – and more aggressive, more assertive and more ego-centred. I should know. I work with guys like that all day! A lot of it is in the upbringing, I suppose. And don't forget our Asian tendency to worship boy children, it's all in the upbringing!"

"Some women claim that it's genetically based – is your fish all right? Good – women carry two X chromosomes, while men carry an X and a Y. The Y chromosome has relatively little genetic information except for what it takes to make a man a man … what this means is that a woman who has a recessive gene on one X chromosome may have a corresponding dominant gene on her other X chromosome … a spare gene, like you may have a spare tire in your car, in case of a breakdown. With only one information-bearing X chromosome, men are more vulnerable to recessive genes that carry biological accidents, and more prone to certain behaviours – although male hormones or androgens don't cause violent or criminally sexual behaviour, they apparently do create an inclination towards it. More male infants die of sudden infant death syndrome, and a much larger proportion of boy children are hyperactive. In adults, this need for extra stimulation seems connected with higher rates of criminal activity."

"It sounds like guys really have things stacked against them. But you can't deny that the way our society is structured, men still get a much better deal."

"So did the Nazis, but they didn't last very long. Think about it."

Jaylin felt that SuFern was watching her for some kind of intelligent reaction. She pushed a sweet nugget of white fish flesh around her plate and ignored the hyperbole.

"It's an interesting idea, but I don't have an opinion on it either way."

"When you said 'female species', something clicked into place. For me, the point of Male Subjugation is that there are no bonding groups for heterosexual men as there are for women and homosexual men. Heterosexual men just don't seem to have any positive role models any more. Neither do they get support for being what they are ... you see, the 'female species' tends to bond easily, whereas every heterosexual man behaves as though he believes he is the sole member of the heterosexual male species."

Jaylin listened. She felt better now that she had eaten something, but her mind still wasn't up to deep conversation.

"I don't understand," she said.

SuFern smiled broadly, as though Jaylin had said something brilliant.

"You see? A heterosexual man couldn't have said that. Not so easily and openly. Not without feeling that he had lost something by saying he didn't understand. Nowadays, when you want to insult a man, you call him a macho shit, an MCP, a typical *Man*. But if you want to say something nice to him, you say that he is wonderfully sensitive ... as sensitive as a woman; you might tell him that he's as thoughtful as a woman, you may tell your friends that he's so gentle with children, or likes poetry or is so good at ironing his own shirts ... it's very difficult to compliment a man on his maleness ... and men who take the best care of their bodies, those bastions of maleness, are assumed to be gay or, worse, totally narcissistic. A man who takes control is labelled an aggressive jerk. A man who doesn't is labelled a spineless wimp."

"Coffee? Tea?" suggested the waiter.

"Tea for two," SuFern told him. To Jaylin she smiled apologetically, "Tea is better for you than coffee."

"Actually I'd like a coffee," Jaylin said mildly.

Their waiter beamed. "One coffee one tea," he said.

"Sorry," said Jaylin, "I need coffee to stay awake."

SuFern shook her head indicating it didn't matter but Jaylin found herself wondering if there was some subtle test involved here. Had she just passed or failed some psychosocial test?

You're getting paranoid, Jaylin.

"It all sounds like a very interesting theory," Jaylin said. "But what does it mean in actual terms? You look around you, there are good guys as well as bad guys. They're all people. And from what I can see, men are still very much in control of things."

"They are in control of things. But they are not comfortable with themselves and *because* they are in control, so to speak, this discord gets passed downwards, affecting more and more people."

"Most men wouldn't care about that."

"So what made them that way? Men didn't create the instincts that made them aggressive, that made them value action over agreement and strength more than sympathy. Nature and human history rewarded those qualities in men and those qualities were necessary, at some stage, to the survival of our species."

Their tea and coffee arrived. Their waiter was still smiling. He served Jaylin with especial care. Jaylin liked him. She also liked SuFern, even though SuFern's theories made for weighty dinner conversation. SuFern's candour was refreshing. She was telling Jaylin things that Jaylin didn't know without making Jaylin feel dumb. At least Jaylin's attention was being diverted from the heavy hopelessness that she had been bogged down in. SuFern's insistent preciseness was something that Jaylin could appreciate.

Jaylin could also appreciate the psychosociologist' s slim back and neat shoulders.

And Dr. Lim SuFern had a way of getting directly to the point.

"How do you feel about men, Jaylin?"

"What a strange question! Not much and not often, I guess. How do you feel about men?"

"I feel that too many men, especially Chinese men, are brought up badly. Because of that it's very difficult to see their true potential. It's sad for them as well as for the people they live and work with."

"I see."

"Not that I can claim to have done any better. I have a son about your age."

"Oh, that's nice. How does he feel about your study?"

"He's not interested in theories. He's a veterinary surgeon. He's a good man, but he's not married yet, so I don't know what kind of husband and father he's going to be."

Jaylin wondered if this was a joke she should laugh at. She gave an amused smile by way of compromise.

"Maybe he hasn't yet met a woman who's been brought up to realise *her* full potential!" she said lightly.

"Yes, I do wonder what sort of woman he's going to marry," SuFern said seriously.

"Jaylin, what sort of man would *you* marry?"

Jaylin took evasive action.

"My father was constantly unfaithful. When I was ten

years old I knew he was having an affair. He moved out to stay with his other woman and told me that he couldn't come home so much because he had to work very hard to make money to buy me nice things. I remember thinking that he was not a very good liar. He came home for my birthday party and then he went back to that woman. I remember all my friends were running around downstairs and Poh Poh was saying, should she light the candles on the cake yet? – and my mother lying in bed upstairs with her face hidden; and I went to lie down beside her and say, don't cry Mummy, Mummy please don't cry … I was glad when he left."

"Your father left your mother?"

"Yes," Jaylin laughed shortly, "I told him to leave, actually. He was probably going to go anyway, but for years I believed that he left because I told him to. We were staying in our old house at Greenfield Drive at that time. I told him 'Go away and don't come back because we don't want you here and we don't need you here!' And you know, actually we didn't. After he left, my mother seemed much happier. We came to stay with Poh Poh Celli and Grandpa Celli in Pasir Panjang. Then a couple of years ago, Mum got her apartment in Orchard Delfi and moved there."

"It's an interesting story," SuFern commented.

"You think so? I guess. But then again, not all men are like my terrible father. Grandpa Celli is wonderful. He's my mother's step-father, but he's been so good to her … he lent her the money to start up her antique shop and within two years she paid it all back. He likes to say that that was the best investment he ever made. Actually, if you're interested in what people make of their lives, you should meet my mum … she really changed so totally once she was on her own."

"I'd very much like to meet your mother. How's your father doing, by the way?"

"All right, I guess. He's still making money, still playing golf, still womanizing."

"You see, your father also recovered from the breakdown of his marriage. He's also doing well at his work and living a full life ... but you don't give him any credit the way you give credit to your mother."

"Well, it was all his fault, wasn't it? He asked for it. It's usually the man's fault, you know. But they can never see it that way."

"Yes, and the fascinating question for psychosociology is why. What makes men this way?"

Jaylin wondered if it was a flash of intuition that prompted her next question: "Did your husband leave you, Dr. Lim?"

SuFern looked as though this was a question she had been asked many times before. But she answered it straight up as it came.

"No. My husband died of a heart attack when he was only forty-five. He was a wonderful man. There's nothing I would like more than to have our son grow up like him, to have more men like him."

"You can't find a scientific formula that produces good men, you know."

SuFern laughed, "I suppose I sound as though that's what I'm trying to do. Really, though, I would just like to find a way for all of us to come to terms with what we've been saddled with. Men have to learn to live with powerful women; women with muscles and anger and intellect. But at the same time, women have to help men to find a way to celebrate manliness without putting it down!"

Behind the News

Behind the news, it was another story altogether.

"I can't understand you, Stephanie, you are being so *silly*!" Mrs. Constance Chen said to her daughter of thirty-four years.

"Why don't you want to come for lunch with us. After all, you must eat something, right? Are you on some sort of hunger strike?"

The confrontation took place in the elegant white-on-white living room of the Chens' luxurious Damansara Heights bungalow.

Stephanie was sitting on a white leather armchair with a sheepskin thrown over it, her long slender legs curled underneath her, while the sisters Constance Chen and Charlotte Goei squarely presented a united front side-by-side on the white leather sofa.

Stephanie was not looking at her mother and her aunt. Stephanie was looking out into the garden.

The Chens employed a good gardener. The wide lawn with its border shrubbery and gracefully positioned trees was lush and well-tended. Looking out, you could not tell that even in February it was warm and humid outdoors, or that the grass was damp underfoot from last night's rain. Viewed through the picture windows from the air-conditioned interior of the living room, it all looked perfect.

It was, after all, scenery meant for looking at rather than living in. And as such, it fulfilled its purpose admirably. It was a picture-perfect garden. Mrs. Chen had put as much thought and effort into designing that view of their garden as she had into choosing any of the paintings that hung in their home.

Some evenings, Mr. Michael Chen practised his golf-swing on the lawn, but his wife did not approve of this because her husband sometimes turned up tufts of grass and earth that marred the perfectness of the view.

Mrs. Chen watched Stephanie looking out into the garden. Stephanie was certainly beautiful, but she wished the girl would make more of an effort to do something *constructive* about herself. All she had done, since that husband of hers had died, was drift aimlessly around the house. And it wasn't even as though they had been a couple of blissfully happy newly-weds. Stephanie didn't even seem to appreciate the fact that Ralph Lake's unfortunate demise had saved them all from the scandal of a divorce. Constance Chen felt more kindly disposed towards her late son-in-law now than she had at any time since Stephanie introduced him into the Chen family.

"Just come out and have lunch with us," Aunt Charlotte urged. "Please, Stephanie. You have to go on with your life, you just have to put all this unpleasant business behind you and go on with your life!"

"After all, you can't stay in here doing nothing forever!" said Constance at her most acerbic.

It was 10 days since Stephanie had set foot out of the house.

Ten days since she had picked up the telephone.

Ten days since she had done anything but sit woodenly and stare woodenly at nothing.

Ten days since she had embarrassed them all by telling the police that she had killed her husband.

It was a good thing that the Malay waitress had been around and could give a *sensible* report of what had really happened.

"I'll eat. I just don't want to go out to lunch," Stephanie said colourlessly.

At last, she finally turned away from the window. But instead of looking at her mother, she looked at the portrait photograph that was framed on the wall above the sofa her parent and aunt were sitting on.

This family portrait had been taken when Stephanie was eleven years old. Her mother and father were sitting side by side on two antique Chinese chairs with Stephanie standing behind and between her parents with one hand on her father's shoulder. Her hair, pulled away from her face in an Alice-in-Wonderland band, fell long and straight and silky over the puffed shoulders of her white dress.

Even then Stephanie had been beautiful.

She had been beautiful and lonely. It was around the time that this photograph was taken that Stephanie had realised the younger brother or sister she had hoped for every year was probably never going to put in an appearance.

"That's a lovely photograph," said Aunt Charlotte, seeing where Stephanie was looking.

Well, Stephanie had not been *entirely* alone. Aunt Charlotte, her devoted aunt and godmother had seen to that, always taking her out shopping and arranging to have little girls come to visit and play with her.

Stephanie's lips smiled at Aunt Charlotte colourlessly and meaninglessly. Otherwise, she remained completely still.

If the girl had been prostrated by grief or distraught with guilt, Mrs. Chen would have found it easier to understand. She could have offered comfort and sympathy and boiled herbal soups. She would have been able to help, to *do* something. It was Stephanie's inertia that Mrs. Chen found most unbearable. Mrs. Chen was one of those women who has to be constantly on the move, *doing* something all the time. She was like one of those little fishes that suffocates on its own gills if it is forced to stay still for too long.

"You can't just stay inside this house forever!" Mrs. Chen said exasperatedly. "It's not healthy, it's not normal, it's abnormal!"

"Where do you want me to go?"

"Anywhere!"

"If there was anywhere I wanted to go to, I would go."

"So, come and have lunch in town with Aunty Charlotte and me!"

"I don't want to."

Constance turned away from her daughter to appeal to her sister, "Aiya! Nei tong kue gong ler! Ngo mo yeh tong kue gong lor!"

Aunty Charlotte clasped her plump hands earnestly together. The rings on her plump fingers glittered her utmost sincerity.

"Stephanie, you know your mother is already so upset over what happened, we have all been so upset over what happened; the only thing to do is to let things get back to normal as quickly as possible!"

What is normal?

Aunty Charlotte leaned forward even more earnestly. Her ample bosom looked in danger of landing on her sister's white marble coffee table.

"Your mother only wants you to come and have lunch with us this one time. This isn't so much to ask, is it? Can't you do it for her? Do it for me?"

Constance straightened her slim back and touched the tip of her tongue to the corners of her mouth. *I have aged very well,* she thought, *don't throw it all away for this silly girl. The main thing to remember* is *not to frown. Frowning stresses your facial muscles and gives you facial lines.*

Daughters give you facial lines.

She smiled resolutely at the cause of her wrinkles.

"Even the police are satisfied that it was an accident. That Malay girl who came in with the drinks also said so. She was a witness; you were both witnesses. So why are you still carrying on like this? It's not as though you were so emotionally attached to that man. The two of you went your separate ways a long time ago! He's gone. Now use your common sense. You can't stay at home all the time without seeing anybody or talking to anyone! You have to get on with your life!"

Constance Chen turned to her sister Charlotte in hopeless exasperation, "She won't even answer her telephone!"

Her sister Charlotte had been told this many times already, but devoted maiden aunts are patient people.

"Maybe she actually did love him," Charlotte suggested to her sister. "After all, he was her husband, she just needs some time to get over it."

"If she wants to be sentimental," stormed Constance, "why can't she be sentimental properly? Why can't she cry like any normal person? Why does she just sit there all the time? It's not natural!"

"Seeing someone die in front of you isn't *natural*," Stephanie said quietly. She wished her father didn't work on Sundays. If her father was around he would have told her mother to leave her alone.

"I cannot talk to this girl at all!" said Stephanie's mother, " – with her sharp tongue and smart mouth!"

"Maybe she needs some time to herself," suggested Aunt Charlotte. "The shock, you know ... the police ... those dreadful reporters ... "

Constance snorted through her elegant nose.

"Why don't you take a little holiday, Stephanie dear," said Aunty Charlotte.

"She *is* on holiday," Constance said impatiently, "her whole life is one long holiday. Maybe if she had to do some work for a change – young people don't know how hard money is to come by these days – "

"Maybe she could go to Singapore for a while. Michael's sister is there, she could stay with her for a while ... it would be a nice change for her, and it would let her get over this quietly ... "

"I could get Michael to telephone Margaret and ask her, I suppose," said Constance, her eyes lighting up.

"She could keep an eye on her ... "

"I don't need anyone keeping an eye on me!" said Stephanie.

But she didn't reject the suggestion of going to Singapore. She liked the idea of going *anywhere* to get away from Kuala Lumpur for a short while. What she really wanted was to get away from herself for a long while.

Home Is Where the Heart Is

"Yes," said Margaret Chen, after a moment's reflection.

"Yes, I think I *will* go to Bali with you."

She smiled at Chin Soon whose round face broke into an even wider smile. He had been trying to persuade Margaret to take this trip with him for weeks. Since she steadily maintained that she was not ready to marry him, and refused to live with him until they were married, Chin Soon treasured these occasional vacation trips as the only time he had Margaret to himself.

Margaret stood up. In shorts, she still had the firm legs of a young girl. 'I'm getting myself some tea. Do you want some?"

Chin Soon was in love with this woman. This falling in love had happened so gradually, in such a prosaic day by day, week by week way, that he had hardly been aware of it until he was more in love with her than he had ever been with anyone or anything in his life up until then. He loved the way she arranged fresh flowers in her shop's antique vases every morning. He loved the way she could be firmly professional yet warm with other antique dealers. He loved the way she laughed at him, the way she handled accounts, the way she made him feel completely at home for the first time in his life.

He loved the way she made him tea.

They were a matched set of rejects, she had joked once.

Margaret's husband had left her, and, nearly 30 years ago, the only other woman Chin Soon had ever loved enough to want to marry had gone off to England without a word to him. She had been a beautiful, shy girl from a rich family; and Chin Soon had always assumed that her family had disapproved of him and spirited her away. Apart from one letter from her telling him that she was fine and that he should not attempt to get in touch with her, he had never seen or heard from her again. It had taken him years to recover from this blow.

When he met Margaret Chen, Chin Soon couldn't imagine how he had come to be so lucky. He thought her ex-husband was a fool to have left her and told her so.

"If that man hadn't left me," Margaret told him, "I wouldn't be the woman I am today. I would just have gone on being a millstone around his neck. Actually I owe him a great deal. The sad thing is, I don't think I'll ever be able to tell him. And in spite of knowing this, I don't think I'll ever be able to forget what he did to me."

It wasn't the man's leaving her that had hurt her so badly. When her husband finally left her (for a woman who left him within a year) Margaret Chen looked around, assessed her situation, and picked herself up. By the time Chin Soon met her, she had patched together her life and her self-esteem. What really hurt her was thinking of the years of her life she had wasted trying to pretend to herself that she believed his feeble excuses, that she didn't notice his womanizing. For the sake of her child, she said. The years of feeling fat and stupid and incompetent and unable to compete with the smart, sexy, career women her husband met through his work. Those years were lost to her forever.

Those years were over. But no matter how much Margaret

said that her ex-husband had done for her in leaving her, Chin Soon knew that if that scumbag ever turned up again, he would personally see to it that he was put down.

Well, perhaps not personally, but he would find someone to see to it. After all, what was the point in having money if you couldn't use it to protect the people you loved?

"Mona can manage the shop on her own until we get back. And besides, I might be able to pick up some things there – "

"We'll have a wonderful time!" he promised. "You'll pick up as many things as you want. But please try to remember, this is supposed to be a holiday."

"I must give Jay a call and let her know I'm going to be out of town … "

Chin Soon was a bit intimidated by Margaret's lesbian daughter.

"She likes you!" Margaret told him again and again, but Chin Soon was not convinced. He was sure Margaret's daughter saw him as an old lecher who was after her young mother. At least the girl didn't *look* like one of those mannish women who never wore makeup and had more hair under their armpits than on their heads. She was a bright girl. Pretty, too. Chin Soon thought that there was still a chance she might meet a nice young man who would cure her of her lesbianism.

On the few occasions they were thrown together, he had enjoyed discussing the advertising business with her. She was quick and sharp and her instincts were good.

If only she had been a man, Chin Soon would have gladly taken her into his own company. Stead-Semple was a respectable company, but you could only go so far with advertising. Peanuts, compared to what Chin Soon could have offered her.

It was a pity Jaylin was only a girl.

If Margaret's husband hadn't been such a bastard the girl would probably have grown up normal and married an acceptable man, and Chin Soon could have given her husband a job in his company. Chin Soon thought ;that Margaret would have liked that.

The phone rang.

Chin Soon waited for Margaret to come round and answer it because she did not like him to answer the telephone in her apartment.

"Yes, yes," Margaret said. Then, sounding concerned, "Oh, oh. Oh dear I No, I didn't know ... no, we didn't hear anything at all!"

He hoped that it was not anything that would interfere with their planned trip to Bali.

"Yes, yes, oh, oh, Oh! How is she feeling? But of course, I understand, of course, of course ... No, I'm sure that's not – oh dear. Really? But the shock – yes, yes, yes, of course, of course, of course ... but how ... ? I see ... well, but if she's not ... oh. No, no, no – no trouble at all ... but I don't know how ... yes, yes, I know, but ... "

Chin Soon watched Margaret on the telephone. She smiled at him apologetically, but he could see that she was upset by the news. What could be happening? He hoped that that daughter of hers wasn't in any trouble. It would be just like her to get mixed up in something. Margaret spoilt that girl. It wasn't her fault, of course. She was naturally soft-hearted and generous, but she spoilt that girl terribly.

"That was my sister-in-law calling from KL."

"Is something wrong? What's wrong?"

He pulled her down to the sofa beside him.

"It's quite terrible. I can't understand why we didn't hear anything ... my niece – my brother's daughter's husband, he had an accident. A fatal accident. And well, naturally, she's upset. Apparently there was some fuss and whatnot going on, some unpleasantness with the police and with reporters ... she wants to get away from KL for a while ... "

"They want to send her here to stay with you, I suppose?"

"Well she shouldn't be *alone* at a time like this. Her aunt, her mother's sister, offered to come down with her but Stephanie won't have it. She wants to be alone. I know exactly how she feels. Your family can be a great support, but sometimes you just want to be alone."

"When is she coming?"

"As soon as possible. They'll see about arrangements and call me back again ... oh my dear, I'm so sorry about Bali. I was really looking forward to it, you know ... "

"So come with me to Bali," Chin Soon said practically. "If your niece needs to get away and be on her own for a while, there's no point you hanging around, is there? Why don't you call your daughter and ask her to keep an eye on her cousin for a couple of days ... You come with me, your niece gets some time to herself, and if anything comes up, she can call Jay. I'm sure Jay will be able to handle anything that comes up!"

Margaret knew from experience that having too-concerned family members around could be a major headache, when you only wanted to be alone.

"Go on, call your daughter."

"Yes, I suppose I could do that. Steffi does sound as though she needs to have some time to herself."

"What happened, anyway?"

"What?"

Margaret was already holding the receiver, waiting for her daughter to pick up the telephone.

"To your niece's husband."

"Some kind of accident. He fell off the balcony in his hotel. I think they should sue the hotel or something. How can they construct balconies that people can fall through just like that? Apparently there was some fuss in the newspapers there and it upset Steffi. It sounds like there isn't anybody home. I wonder where they've all gone to. I wonder why we didn't hear anything about it here?"

Margaret put down the telephone and dialled again.

"There was this American chap who was supposed to be getting back to us about a business deal ... he fell off a balcony in Kuala Lumpur some time last week. That was also in some hotel ... "

"American businessman? Steffi's husband was American? They were separated or something. I suppose they may have been trying to get back together again when this happened ... "

"It was in the newspapers last week, I think it was in the papers; yes, I read about it in the newspapers last week. I was wondering why he hadn't got back to us and then I found out that he had killed himself ... "

"Hello Ma? It's Margaret. How are you? Oh ... is Jay home? The thing is, I just heard that Steffi may be coming down to Singapore for a couple of days, yes ... well, it's a

60

long story. No, that wife of his called … she said it was all Michael's idea … the thing is, I'm going to be in Bali for a few days – "

Chin Soon smiled.

" – her husband died, apparently. Yes, I also thought they were … but she's very upset by the whole business … when? Oh, I'm probably leaving before this weekend … Yes, that would be nice! After all, they're about the same age. You want *me* to tell her. All right. I'll have her over for dinner before I leave … oh, who's this friend of hers?"

Another girlfriend? Chin Soon wondered.

Girls these days were shameless.

Later, when he asked Margaret about that she only said, "I'd like Jay to find someone. You know, it's hard being alone, especially when you're growing older. I don't even care if it is a man or a woman any more, I would just like her to find a nice person who will be good to her … they can grow old together, and if they decide to adopt a child I can help them to look after it."

And what about the shop? Chin Soon wondered. Margaret had these grandmotherly yearnings every once in a while. He decided to distract her.

"I'll try to find that old issue of the newspaper for you. I'm sure there's a copy lying around in the office some-where … "

What The New Paper Said

American tourist and businessman Ralph Emerson Lake, 30, originally of New York City, in Kuala Lumpur hoping for a reconciliation with his estranged wife, fell to his death from his room in The Executive Spa yesterday.

His widow, local girl Madam Stephanie Chen Lay Hoon, 35, witnessed the accident. In a state of shock, all she could say was, "I killed him, I killed him."

Various members of her family made no comment.

There were unconfirmed reports of Ralph Lake entertaining prostitutes in his hotel room in which there was a strong smell of alcohol. There was also broken glass and evidence that a struggle of some sort had taken place shortly before tragedy struck.

A spokesman of the hotel denied the report, but admitted that it was possible that such goings-on could have taken place without the hotel's knowledge.

Police are interviewing prostitutes and chambermaids.

See box for report on other American tourists who have recently fallen to their deaths under suspicious circumstances in Malaysian hotels.

Papaya Farms

"So you actually knew this guy?"

The tall, broad-shouldered man in a blue polo T-shirt folded the newspaper over its small photograph of the late Ralph Lake, and the larger photograph of the late Ralph Lake's widow and her father hiding their faces behind newspapers, and considered the question put to him.

"Well, yes ... I suppose you could say he was a friend – "

Steve Thurairatnam was a man of upright moral character. He was an affectionate and dutiful son who lived with his widowed (Chinese) mother; and an honest citizen who never punched out his URA/HDB parking coupons more than five minutes in advance of Singapore Standard Time.

But he lied when he said that the late Ralph Lake had been a friend ...

Dr. Steve Thurairatnam had been serving his study bond at the National University of Singapore's Institute of Molecular and Cell Biology when Ralph Lake presented himself as a foreign consultant on learning skills.

Steve had been one of those assembled in a committee to discuss what Mr. Lake had to offer (enthusiasm, originality, a new perspective, experience on other projects, a desire to live in Singapore for a while and improve Singapore to Singapore's great benefit ...).

The panel's decision had already been made in favour of another candidate when Steve, playing the hospitable Singaporean host, invited Ralph Lake out to dinner and drinks. In confident ignorance, Ralph Lake talked about how well he and Steve were going to get along once they were working together. Given his help, Ralph Lake said, confidently, Steve could really make something of his career.

Steve felt like a fraud because he could not say "No, we're not going to be working together," but it was not his place to do so.

Over dinner, Ralph Lake had also talked about his beautiful Malaysian third wife (Chinese; skin like porcelain, body like a porn star's; daughter of a very important, very prominent Malaysian family) who was utterly devoted to him. She was frigid, of course, like all Chinese women. She wore her frigidity like a chastity belt that protected her virtue from the advances of other men. Travelling on the job allowed Ralph Lake all the freedom he needed, smug in the knowledge that his wife would be chastely waiting for him when he returned.

Ralph Lake had assumed the role of mentor to Steve Thurairatnam. Steve, in defiance of government policy, was still single.

"An open relationship, absolute honesty but no ties, no restrictions," Ralph Lake had said proudly and modestly.

"It's the only way a marriage can survive. Take it from someone who knows!

"You know what advice my ex-wife gave me? She said, 'When you're in Asia, only do it with virgins, that way you know that they're clean.' She was one sharp lady, I can tell you that. South American. But she was more American than me like that!" Ralph Lake snapped his fingers, "I didn't like that, I can tell you! You ready for another one? It's on me. Hey, waiter! Garçon!"

Ralph Lake's shrill giggle of little boy conspiracy was starting to give Steve a headache.

"Women. Pick 'em out of the States and keep 'em out of the States, that's my advice to you. You guys know how to handle women in your culture, I'll give you that. In their place. Right there ... "

Ralph Lake pointed down at his crotch and giggled again, nudging Steve with his elbow.

Steve noticed, with the detachment of an anthropologist, that the man's elbows were clothed in Armani.

There were men even Armani couldn't work miracles on.

Steve Thurairatnam wondered what made Ralph Lake attractive to women. Did that raspy, high pitched voice arouse some submerged maternal urge in women? Did short, balding, paunchy men remind them of their fathers?

Or did some post-colonial women still believe a white man's sperm impregnated them with class ... ? Without ever meeting Ralph Lake's Malaysian third wife, Steve Thurairatnam knew that she had to be some ditzy, brainless, Sarong Party Girl.

What can you do when the Ralph Lakes of the world ask you point blank what the night life around Singapore is like? You can't tell them that your idea of a really great night is a good run followed by a workout at Clark Hatch and a grilled fish dinner at Parrots with the latest issue of Scientific American or PC Magazine, can you?

Maybe he should have done that. The next time he would do that.

"Another one for you, buddy? Steve, you still with me? Come on, this one's on me."

Ralph Lake wanted something from him or through him, Steve had already sensed that; and he was trying to get in on the old buddy-buddy basis. Steve didn't really care. It was all part of the job. He hadn't had too much to drink, but he was deliberately blearing out so that Ralph Lake's night entertainment spiel washed harmlessly over his head.

"Let me tell you about these papaya farms," Ralph Lake said with all the avidity of a small boy getting down to share a smutty joke at last.

Papaya farms, thought Steve, how nice. Steve was thinking about *Carica papaya*. It was a plant that he was fond of.

Though people talk about papaya trees, Carica papaya is barely a tree, since its palm-like trunk, which can grow up to eight metres tall, is not as woody as that of a typical tree. It is a dioecious species, male and female flowers being produced on separate plants; but hermaphroditic forms are known, and numerous irregularities in the distribution of the sexes are common.

Steve had graduated with a degree in Veterinary Sciences from Murdoch University, but his major passion was plant life forms. Musing on the sexual irregularities of the papaya plant was a happy distraction from which he was hauled back unceremoniously by Ralph Lake who misread the look of beatific joy on Steve's face.

Ralph's papaya farms were not quite the papaya farms that Steve had in mind.

"Calling such places papaya farms is a great crosscultural joke," Ralph squeaked, perhaps a little too loudly. A couple at a nearby table looked at them distastefully.

"A successful cross-cultural joke, perhaps the only successful cross-cultural joke that both the Cantonese and the Aussies could understand!"

But Steve, born in Ipoh and educated in Perth, still hadn't got the world's one successful cross-cultural joke.

"You know papayas?" Ralph peered raucously into Steve's bleariness.

"A spherical to cylindrical fruit," said Steve, playing it straight down the line.

"Seventy-five to 500 millimetres or even more in length, sometimes weighing as much as 11 kilograms. They characteristically have very juicy flesh, deep yellow or orange to reddish salmon. Along the walls of the large, central cavity you find attached round, black seeds. Papayas are usually grown from seed. Their development is rapid, fruit being produced before the end of the first year."

Somewhere along the way, Ralph Lake had lost track of the conversation. But being an entrepreneur, he waited until he saw a break and plunged in.

He plunged in now, with both hands, "So what do you think of this, eh?"

To Steve, it looked as if Ralph was squeezing two huge, hanging balls of putty. Steve realised, of course, that there was something lewd involved.

"Well, what do you think? How about it, eh?"

Ralph Lake panted up at him like a small puppy and all but wagged his little tail.

"You have naked women picking the papayas?"

This had brought on fits of giggles that Ralph Lake tried, unsuccessfully, to turn into guffaws.

"There aren't any papaya trees! There aren't any papayas. Steve, you don't know anything about your own culture, let me tell you. What do papayas remind you of? Think, Stevie Boy! The good old Aussie pawpaw ... Steve, you're putting me on!"

Steve wasn't putting him on. He was genuinely fond of the papaya plant.

"Come down with me some weekend and I'll show you around! Whaddya doing tomorrow night?"

"Sorry, Ralph, I'm not up to it."

"Heh, you carry on like that and people are going to think that you're queer!"

Steve Thurairatnam stared down Ralph's giggle.

Ralph's face sobered up, a hint of apprehension creeping in.

"Actually, I prefer to say 'gay', myself," Steve said coldly. "Excuse me, I have to get home to my mother."

Ralph Lake and Steve Thurairatnam never met again. Steve left the IMCB and had no reason to call the man to mind until he read about his death in the newspapers.

Which is why, when Steve Thurairatnam was asked, that afternoon in February, whether he had known the late Ralph Lake, he was not quite honest in calling him a friend.

He may, however, be forgiven for trying to speak well of the dead. He even managed to be sorry at the news of the man's death, *poor guy, what a way to go*. Steve Thurairatnam hadn't really known the dead man very well.

Not well enough to know that Ralph Lake had announced to anyone interested in hearing him out that he had lost that job in Singapore he had been *promised* after he turned down a pass made by Steve Thurairatnam.

"When I turned him down, that was it. He wasn't capable of making any other decision. He went against the whole panel and convinced them to hire someone else because he couldn't bear to have me working there with him after I turned him down. But it turned out to be a good thing too. You never know where you are, working with these queers. You can't trust them, you can't believe anything they say."

Even Stephanie Lake, *nee* Chen, believed that Steve Thurairatnam was a homosexual who had gone out of his way to prevent her husband from getting a job that had been promised to him in Singapore.

Walkman and Woman

The shortest month of the year was rapidly beginning to feel like one of the longest in Lee Jaylin's life.

For one thing, her car was still in the garage. Jaylin was well aware that tens of thousands of Singaporeans managed to function each day on public transport; but knowing this wasn't much help as yet another occupied taxi flashed past her and her briefcase grew heavier and her shoes tighter during the course of her walk to the bus stop or MRT station. Being temporarily without her car forced Lee Jaylin to face one fact: successful executive or not, somewhere along the line she had lost something. Somewhere along the way she had gone soft and become addicted to her creature comforts.

During her schooldays, the young Jaylin had thought nothing of carrying a far heavier schoolbag (plus water bottle, plus plastic bag with PE equipment, plus Art Block, plus pack of bubble gum, plus homemade five stones) over far greater distances without the benefit of either umbrella or sunglasses. Even the steep gradient up Mount Sophia had left her unfazed in those days. She and her friends would run down Adis Road to buy sheets of gaudy stickers and clear plastic packets of wrinkled sours. Or they would buy ice-cream. The no-brand ice cream seller, wearing his hat and singlet and with his cigarette dangling from the corner of his mouth, would slice a generous inch of ice cream off his long, rectangular paper-wrapped block with a satisfying swish and thud of his cleaver. He peeled the thin strip of paper off your block of ice-cream after clapping it between thin vanilla wafers; or you might choose to eat your ice-cream tucked inside a slice of white bread instead.

Of course, all this was strictly contraband. In those days, people still worried about cholera and dysentery. But Jaylin and her friends had survived the experience to grow up healthy. And perhaps their disobedience had enriched them beyond what any lesson in Health Science could do.

Where had she gone? That gay girl-child with an appetite for home-made ice cream, batter-fried kachang, keropok, salted lime peel, jelly sweets, and goreng pisang even on the hottest of days? Had she really turned into this woman who would rather skip lunch than face the steamy heat of the world outside her office? Who would rather stay in her office till seven, eight, nine at night to escape the homeward commuter rush?

But Jaylin knew that she wasn't the only person who felt certain that the world had become a far hotter place since her childhood days. She believed there was scientific data proving this, though she couldn't have quoted the exact source ... but contemporary schoolchildren seemed to be braving the heat as effortlessly as she once had, so the resiliency of youth probably had something to do with it too. And possibly more than Jaylin would have liked to think about.

But at the moment, Jaylin had more pressing problems on her mind. The day before, one of her account executives had crashed into a major stress breakdown right there in the Stead-Semple office.

His brief but violent outbreak had left the office with

three smashed glass partitions, and Jaylin had inherited a presentation scheduled for 11:30 A.M. two days later.

The broken glass had been cleared away, the partitions had been measured and replaced within a day of the incident; the state of the unfortunate executive's mental health and the overwhelming stress of working in the advertising agency had been discussed and rediscussed at fashionable luncheon niches throughout the Central Business District ... and Lee Jaylin was still working at putting together the presentation that had been so suddenly thrust into her lap.

She was not out to create an extraordinarily striking and memorable presentation. She was not even looking for a great presentation, demonstrating Stead-Semple's standards of effortless excellence ...

Lee Jaylin had reached a stage where all she was looking for was a way – any way – to pull things together and save some face for Stead-Semple.

And why was she doing this ... out of loyalty to her company?

Or because she believed that it would be made worth her while, where her future with the company was concerned?

Or because she was doing nothing more important or interesting with her life at that point in time?

Or because it didn't seem likely that she would *ever* be doing anything more important or interesting with her life?

Though she didn't realise it, Jaylin was longing for something to happen in her life, something to give it meaning and justification. If she had been a married woman, she would probably have craved a baby of her own as an object she could devote her whole life to. If she had been a single, happily heterosexual woman, she would have craved a husband, to fulfill the same function. As too many women are aware, such relief is only temporary, but as too few women will admit, you have to try it before you know if you like it.

Jaylin, being Jaylin, tried to immerse herself totally in her work. But even when she was successful, this was not very satisfactory. She sat in front of a desk spread over with papers and project files and wondered if she should get a dog, or think about spending a year as a volunteer of some sort in some place like Nicaragua.

Even her faithful Mun Ee had departed at 8:30 P.M. after quietly putting two char siew pows and a banana on Jaylin's desk. Mun Ee had a husband at home who might or might not still remember her after all the overtime she had been putting in at work.

Looking out through the wide panes of the windows behind her, she could see a myriad lights shining from the towers of glass and concrete that surrounded her, high in the night sky. Each light signified at least one lonely soul doggedly, perhaps desperately, in pursuit of some ephemeral goal. And yet the sight of those quiet, watchful lights still gave her a frisson of heady excitement. There was something encouragingly enduring in this good darkness that hid no rioting, no terrorism, no slums. Their goals might be ephemeral but their drive, their devotion, their persistent perfectionism, these things would endure.

She was proud to be a part of her tribe.

Life in the fast lane is both more and less than it is made out to be. Generally, when seen close up, it is more stress and less glamour. Yet there is a certain dignity – just as there is dignity in the caged mouse who holds his head up high as he runs endlessly, endlessly on his treadmill.

David Dillon had left only the sketchiest of notes for the Tuesday morning meeting. Everything else had been in his head or scribbled in indecipherable notes, Mun Ee told Jaylin, and his head was a basket case at the moment. Nobody really knew what had snapped or why. His wife was flying him straight back to London.

In a straitjacket, Jaylin hoped.

Jaylin's first (admittedly unworthy) response had been to suspect David Dillon had played himself out in Batam over the weekend; that there were *no* details in his head; and that his collapse was an artistic invention designed to distract attention from his negligence.

Now she felt guilty for maligning him in her thoughts. Poor Mercy Dillon. Surely no one would fly all the way to London just to substantiate an alibi? Still, Jaylin hoped they strapped his straitjacket on tight. He had no business getting away scot free while she slaved away here in his place.

Don't go overboard, Jaylin!

The British were still the most conscientious expatriates to work with (and David Dillon had a very nice Sri Lankan wife to keep his feet on the ground. Jaylin *liked* Mercy Dillon); but except for the Methodist missionaries Jaylin remembered from her early days in a mission school, all the white expatriates she had worked with were prone to MLW, the 'More to Life than Work' syndrome that the average Singaporean finds so difficult to comprehend.

Of course those original missionaries, more than anyone else, believed that there was more to life than keeping up with the rat race. But though they might consider themselves humble workers with an eye on the next realm, they also worked harder than anyone else in this one.

Effort-wise, they were nicely in keeping with the wholesome Singaporean overwork ethic.

Jaylin had already roughed out the main points of the Stead-Semple proposal. That part was easy. It was the details, the fine-tuning, the final touches, the custom fit that Stead-Semple was so famous for, that she needed to work out now.

And she was sitting there feeling brain dead. She had made no progress for the past 45 minutes.

Of course, she could have left, it as it was and gone home. She could have gone home and had a hot shower and gone to bed. She could have gone home safe in the assurance that the sun would rise on Shenton Way whether or not the proposal was perfect and complete.

But where would that leave Lee Jaylin?

Jaylin suspected that if she allowed herself to let go of her self-imposed standards just once, it would signal the start of a long and frightening slide downhill. Once she started sliding, where would it all end?

Oh, the endless insecurity of conscientious people ... be warned, Gentle Reader. If you ever find yourself at a point in your life where your ability to do the job well becomes more important to you than either the job itself or you and all your other abilities, it is time to take a long, hard look at yourself and the life you are living.

Perhaps Jaylin sensed the yawning gulf between the life she was living and the life she might have chosen for herself. Too wide a gulf at too inappropriate a time can lead to madness. Was that what had happened to David Dillon? So Lee Jaylin shut that door in her mind and sat at her desk in her well lit office. She looked at the papers on the desk in front of her.

She looked at the office around her. As long as she was still sitting there, she could convince herself that she was still hard at work. The plastic plants flourished luxuriantly in their glass planters full of plaster beads; the Mondrian prints were pristine on the uncracked glass walls; Jaylin's ankles were crossed on her desk; her shoes abandoned on the thick pile carpet ...

With a small sigh of surrender, Jaylin reached behind her for another can of Pepsi-Cola. She told herself that she needed the caffeine to keep her alert. At this rate even she was going to start putting on weight soon. She could visualise how the *Singapore Tatler* would run the expose if it ever came up.

Lee Jaylin, top Advertising Executive with Stead-Semple, is addicted to Pepsi. Our interviewer asked Lee Jaylin the question that everyone has been dying to ask:

"Isn't it just a bit humiliating to have a vice that isn't even as dangerous as it is fattening?"

"I've never really had a problem with weight," Lee Jaylin, comfortable at 260 pounds, says confidently.

So far her vivid mental screenplays had not succeeded in scaring her off the carbonated, caffeinated, artificially sweetened booze.

Jaylin turned up the volume on her CD player. At least she could drown out the sound of her fat cells bloating up on simple sugars. She was listening to Mitsuko Uchida play Mozart's Piano Concertos 24 and 25 with the English Chamber Orchestra, conducted by Jeffrey Tate. Music always provided a good background for drowning her immediate problems.

David Dillon had liked music too.

Jaylin made a note to herself: *remember to ask Mun Ee*

to telephone Mercy Dillon in London tomorrow and ask how her husband is doing.

Jaylin wanted to phone somebody herself, but she couldn't think of anyone to call.

If only Gerry was still in Singapore, Jaylin could have picked up the phone and called her at home or at Hewlett-Packard and Gerry would either have come down to keep her company in the office or they could have arranged to meet for a drink after they finished their respective tasks. Having something to look forward to always makes it easier to persevere through a long evening's work. And Gerry could always find a way to make them laugh at the ridiculous way they were pushing themselves ...

But who knew where Gerry was by now?

The woman was mad ...

"One day I'll wake up and realise that I'm old and my life is over," Gerry had said. "This way, when the time comes, I'll be able to say, I may be old and my life may be over, but I've been to San Francisco, Morocco, Greece, Nepal ... "

"Gerry, when you're old what difference will it make whether you've been to San Francisco or not?"

"Maybe no difference at all. But I don't want to be too old to travel and stuck in my wheelchair wondering whether or not it would have made a difference, so I'm going) I wish you would change your mind and come with me!"

"I can't afford it."

"Of course you can!"

Of course, neither of them had really expected Jaylin to do anything so drastic. Jaylin was the sensible one, the practical one ...

The really depressing thing for Jaylin was that up until then, everyone who knew them would have assumed that Geraldine Lai was equally sensible and practical. Only her expensive weakness for *Ken Done* T-shirts had suggested a yearning for a more colourful life.

Was Gerry's sudden restlessness something that attacked middle-aged, successful, unmarried, executive women when they least expected it?

And was this how middle age would make itself felt, when Jaylin least expected it?

Unexpectedly, Jaylin found herself wondering what Gerry would have thought of SuFern. SuFern was even more rational and logical than Jaylin herself. SuFern must have dealt with the coming of middle age in her own way, because she was still gracefully and gainfully employed and still seemed excited by the work she was doing. It would be interesting to introduce Gerry to SuFern. The thought made Jaylin smile.

She was so tired. This was what happened when you skipped dinner and under-charged your system with over-refined sugars. The two pows that Mun Ee had left her still sat coldly, fatly white and faintly reproachful on her desk. Even the cool smoothness of the beadily-wet aluminium can failed to raise Jaylin's spirits.

It had not been a good day.

It was not a good night.

And there was nothing to suggest things would be getting any better ...

Knock, knock.

"Hello there ... "

A less poised executive would have spilled her Pepsi down her front. Jaylin's reflexes saved her. There, in Jaylin's doorway, stood Dr. Lim SuFern, looking fresh and uncrushed in a grey skirt with a green weave and a pale pink short-sleeved blouse with a carnation pearl pin at the throat. Her short, grey hair was immaculately in place, and even from where she was, Jaylin caught a faint murmur of *White Linen*.

Jaylin instantly felt crumpled, grimy, greasy and very end-of-the-day.

"Sorry if I startled you, Jaylin. One of your colleagues directed me here. Is this the night shift or does everyone in Stead-Semple work a 24-hour day?" Jaylin was pleased to see a friendly face, though embarrassed to be caught (literally) with her shoes off. She took her ankles off the table and sat up straight as a proper executive should. She knew that she had probably shattered the myth of the poised, impeccable, implacable Advertising Executive, but she wasn't at all sorry to see Dr. Lim again.

"Walkmans," said SuFern in a severe, motherly tone, "are so bad for your ears!"

"It's not a Walkman. It's a Discman, and it's not switched on ... "

Jaylin took off her ear plugs. The Mozart had come to an end without her noticing.

"Ah I suppose that's all right, then," SuFern sat down on one of the glass and leather chairs on the other side of Jaylin's desk and smiled at her.

"You think I'll live, then?"

"There's a good chance you will – I hope so, anyway!"

"What are you doing here?"

"I thought I might find you here, you weren't at home and

your grandmother said that she thought you were working late – "

"You called me at home? What was it about?"

"I wanted to show you some preliminary notes I've written up on what we discussed the other night. I've quoted you – no names used, of course – and I would like to know what you think ... have you got time now or shall I leave it with you?"

"I'll read it now. I was about to call it a night, anyway!"

"Is your car out of the garage yet?"

"No ... I was just about to call a cab."

"Don't. I'll give you a ride home."

"You don't have to ... "

"My pleasure. Actually I have an ulterior motive. There are just a couple more questions I was hoping to ask you. Do you know you're almost impossible to reach during the day?"

"I have a very efficient assistant!"

SuFern switched off the air-conditioning in the car when they were far enough south to catch the salt breeze coming off the night sea. From Pasir Panjang Highway they could see lights and moving figures in the warehouses and dockside buildings. Further out, over the water, the distant ship's lights shone small and steadily yellow over the water.

Jaylin felt a twinge of apprehension for her contact lenses (had it really been so long since she'd been in a car without air-conditioning on?) as the wind whipped into the car. She edged her window up a centimetre. She could feel her lenses drying out even as she thought about them. She had her sunglasses in her purse, of course, but to put them on at this time of night would have moved her a couple of steps beyond eccentricity.

Jaylin was feeling cross with herself. She wasn't sure exactly why. Because she felt that she was petty to worry about her contacts yet couldn't stop thinking about her contacts? Because she didn't like to be sitting in the passenger seat being driven home by someone else because her car had broken down? Or perhaps just because she was tired, and tired people frequently feel cross and cranky with no real justification.

But Jaylin had sat through a sufficient number of long and undirectioned meetings not to let her feelings show in her face. Working for Stead-Semple had taught her the art of personal PR, if nothing else. When they stopped for a red light and watched an enormous container roll out across their path, SuFern gestured towards the lights out on their left.

"All this used to be sea, can you remember? Or maybe you are too young to remember. Are you? All this used to be sea, and then they reclaimed it. All those houses over there on our right used to be beachfront property. Wide stone steps leading down to the garden and the garden leading down to the beach. Now there's an expressway between them and the water. And when you get to the water it's full of commercial traffic."

"That's progress," said Jaylin with the off-handed snidism unthinkingly assumed by so many of those brought up on the benefits of that progress.

"It was necessary," said SuFern seriously, "but still, it's sad. With the extra land we got the building space that we needed, we got the port space that we needed, but we lost beach space. And we have no tangible way of measuring how much we lost when we lost our beaches."

"There's always Sentosa. Artificial beaches with imported sand that's whiter and finer than our own."

"Well, we're all imported people. We can be happy on imported beaches!"

Jaylin laughed. She relaxed, even though the sea breeze rushed into the moving car. They passed tankers, with their tiny lights and deep booms, as they lay companionably in the dark, deep waters.

"We're all island people, whether we realise it or not. We need to know that the sea is there around us, close around us. One of my colleagues was studying in America. He said he didn't realise how homesick he could be for water until he found himself completely land bound for months ... then he and some other Singaporeans drove a few hundred miles just to get to the Great Lakes. That was the nearest water, the ocean was even further off. But he needed that. America is so enormous; there's so much land between its coasts. After he told me that, I realised that I've always taken for granted having water nearby. Island people need water. Singaporeans are island people, all our ancestors came here out of the sea ... "

"Like my grandmother," Jaylin said, breathing in the good sea air, beginning to look around her with opening eyes. "She came by sea ... "

Poh Poh

Poh Poh, Jaylin's grandmother, the first woman in her province to get a university degree, ran away from her wealthy family home in Szechuan to join the revolution.

However, the revolution (like all the preceding and subsequent revolutions) failed to create the new China she and all the other students dreamt of and marched for so she married a fellow revolutionary and they went out into the world to find a future for themselves. They were in Malaya when the Second World War reached Southeast Asia. Chen Jen Tai joined the resistance. He was caught and tortured to death by the Japanese.

Taken, with her young son and baby daughter, to look at his butchered body, his wife managed to convince the soldiers that she did not recognise him.

They survived the war. The British gave Chen Jen Tai a posthumous award for valour. Poh Poh wasted no energy on bitterness, but she did not allow Japanese toys, electronic equipment, or instant noodles in the house. She also would not sit in a Japanese made car, which could make hailing taxis a tricky business.

Poh Poh supported and educated her children on her salary as a mathematics and geography teacher in the Methodist Boys' School in Ipoh. Those were hard times, but her children were always clean and neat, even if their clothes were hand-me-downs. They were bright children, and she was very strict with them, believing in the paramount importance of education. She wouldn't even let them help around the house; she thought it was more important for them to study. Poh Poh tried to make sure that they both got a university education, but six months after her daughter went to Singapore to study in what was then known as the University of Malaya, she announced that she was dropping out of the university and getting married. Poh Poh rushed South, met her daughter's husband-to-be and worried very much over her daughter's future ...

"But what's to stop you from finishing your degree first? Or continuing with your course after you're married?"

Of course there was nothing to stop the girl from going on with her education, but Margaret got married and pregnant instead of finishing her course at the university because her husband didn't think that he needed a wife with a degree. After all, he didn't have one himself. He wasn't marrying her for her brains.

Poh Poh worried that it was growing up without a father that had driven her daughter into an early and possibly unwise marriage. However, there was nothing that she could do about it, except hope that all would turn out well.

Poh Poh's son dutifully got his degree and married an ex-beauty queen who was also an accomplished cook. He had always been a level-headed child. He and his new wife settled down in Kuala Lumpur, where he launched a stable, secure career, and they looked forward to starting a family.

Then after both her children were married and she had fulfilled and discharged her responsibilities as a parent, Poh Poh surprised everybody by moving down to Singapore and getting married again herself.

Robert Celli was a widower with grown-up children. He had lied in Singapore for over 20 years, arriving after the war with the military and finding he liked the country too well to leave it with the coming of Independence.

Poh Poh and Robert Celli were a very happy couple. They walked straight into the best years of marriage, having come together only after the stress and struggle of raising families was safely behind them.

Years later, when Poh Poh's daughter was abandoned by her husband, Poh Poh thought, *marriage is wasted on the young, and on people in a hurry* ... She managed, just barely managed, not to say 'I told you so'. By then, her daughter had lived through enough to learn her lesson several times over.

Jaylin had been a flower girl at Poh Poh's second wedding; and she had been a flower girl in a singlet and panties because minutes before the procession down the aisle of Wesley Methodist Church, she managed to strip off the itchy white dress and the scratchy flowers wired to her hair.

Her grandmother, never one to value ceremony over spontaneity, only laughed.

"You can't walk down with Poh Poh without your dress on!" her mother chided her.

"Of course she can!" her grandmother, the blushing bride, insisted.

Jaylin did, however, carry her tiny bouquet of yellow rosebuds. Poh Poh bribed her Jay-Jay to put her dress back on for the photograph taking session, offering her a choice between a five dollar note and a 10 dollar note.

Jay-Jay took the 10. Even then she had had an eye for getting ahead.

Poh Poh's son and daughter-in-law came down from KL for her wedding, but they didn't bring their daughter with them. Stephanie didn't travel very well, the ex-beauty queen explained to her mother-in-law.

"My sister is looking after her."

Poh Poh would have liked to have both her granddaughters at her wedding, but she didn't feel comfortable enough with her daughter-in-law to insist. Poh Poh felt that in the younger woman's eyes, the words *practically senile* were hovering above her head throughout the marriage ceremony. Mrs. Constance Chen obviously felt it wasn't quite *proper* for people of their advanced years to be getting married ... certainly not in a church with granddaughters serving as bridesmaids.

But if not now, then when?

They weren't going to get any younger by waiting!

After the wedding ceremony, Poh Poh's daughter-in-law took it upon herself to ask the newly-weds if they had thought about making wills ... after all, you couldn't be too careful, and at *their* age ... it was always better to be prepared for everything, wasn't it?

"If it's going to be a problem," Robert Celli told his new daughter-in-law happily, "we'll make sure that we spend it all before we go! Won't you have more champagne, my dear?"

The Cellis were a very happy couple in their marriage. Retired on comfortable pensions, theirs was an idyllic life. They lived by the sea in a raised, white plaster bungalow along Pasir Panjang Road. Dwarf coconut palms grew around the perimeter of the fence and travellers palms and jasmine bushes lined the long driveway. At night, the frangipani trees scented the cricket cries in the air, and in season there were rambutans and chempedak from the trees in the back garden.

There was a little house behind the big house, where the gardener and the house servant had lived when they still had a gardener and house servant. The last of each had long since passed away. The pandan leaves, serai, mint, and curry-leaf tree planted around the little house by those long-gone hands still flourished, now joined by climbing, twisting, tangling trails of morning glory.

Poh Poh made her will in 1988. In her will she left the graceful little Pasir Panjang house to her granddaughter Jaylin, with the proviso that she should not sell it to condominium developers, but live in it herself for as long as that should prove practical.

There were so many years of quiet happiness within the simple, white walls of that house.

There Will Always Be a Raffles

There will always be a Raffles Multiplex, Jaylin thought wryly.

Jaylin had started her day chirpily enough. Talking with SuFern the night before had restored some balance to her perspective on life. She enjoyed the earnest seriousness with which SuFern considered everything, even matters which Jaylin would not normally have found worth considering. Yet her seriousness was never grim. Nor did SuFern have that air of busy-busy-business which so many modern Singaporeans find an indispensable accessory.

Yet Jaylin suspected that SuFern accomplished much in her apparently aimless manner.

Jaylin had talked and laughed and loosened some of the tension coiled inside her. Then, with a calm mind, she had slept well and woken refreshed, early enough to take time for a short chat with her grandmother over her morning coffee and still get into the office in plenty of time.

She was going through her day's schedule when, as on so many mornings, the first call of her day came from Mrs. Maria Fernandez Gong.

Was the good feeling too good to last?

Maria had called to tensely, jaw-clenchedly, tightthroatedly whine, complain and assert that Stead-Semple was not providing her with the kind of service that she had expected of a firm of their reputation.

Maria, you've always had this habit of always expecting too much, it's time to get real, girl!

Of course Jaylin didn't say that. For one thing, Maria was now a client.

For another thing, Maria had a tendency to take such comments personally. Jaylin knew Maria well enough to know that Maria would brood over her comment if she had made it, and would arrive, some months later, at the startling conclusion that Jaylin believed that Maria was disappointed in her children or in her (much complained about) marriage to Gerald Gong.

Over Maria's insistent lament, Jaylin could hear a child's voice wailing in the background. Maria was calling from home, then. This call, like so many others, was to be logged into Maria's work record to show that Maria had not been late into the office ... she had been busy working, making her calls from home.

Maria herself had admitted that she was disappointed and disillusioned. She was, however, uncertain whether she was disillusioned with Gerald Gong in particular or with the state of Holy Matrimony in general. Should she have married someone else? Should she not have married at all? But all this was only to exercise her imagination. Maria had been brought up a good Catholic woman, and remained a good Catholic woman.

There was nothing she could do about her marital situation now, except to make sure that her husband was as miserable in wedlock as she was.

Listening to Maria made Jaylin glad that *she* wasn't married. In particular, it made her glad that she wasn't married to Maria Fernandez Gong.

"The Japanese don't want yet another posh hotel-cum-shopping complex. They want something *different* some totally *new* – I promised them that you would come up with a completely revolutionary concept and you come up with service apartments? You call this new? How can you do this to me, Jaylin? After all the years we've been friends, I thought you'd put a bit more thought into this."

Let's not get personal here, all right Maria? Let's not go into what we'd do in the name of friendship, OK?

"I thought you wanted a safe bet," Jaylin said patiently. "You said you wanted this to be a sure thing, a no-risk venture … "

"Well … "

You could always tell, thought Jaylin, when someone was insecure on the job, by the way they tried to talk their way around the most minor situation without losing face.

A simple "I've changed my mind," or "Is that the impression I gave? It's not the impression I meant to give," would have been that much more succinctly impressive.

Some people never learn that. They are the people who remain forever on the lower rungs of life, making perfect excuses.

"I can't give you something that's tried and true and at the same time totally original," Jaylin was saying to Maria when she caught the *perfect excuse* note in her own voice and was shocked into sudden silence.

You know that you're in trouble when you put more effort into coming up with reasons why a project won't work than into making the project work.

And she, Jaylin, was beginning to do just that.

It's time to take off for a break in the Maldives.

Or since there's no one to take off for a break in the Maldives with, maybe it's just time to sit up straight and really dig around for a way to break through the problem.

One maxim Jaylin had learned years ago from her mathematics tutor in Anglo-Chinese Junior College still stood her in good stead: *if you can't solve a problem, then you should prove it insoluble.*

In other words, there is always an answer, even if it is not the answer that you have been looking for. It was funny how the philosophy remained Jong after the mathematics had gone. Perhaps that was the true point of education.

"I'll get back to you," Jaylin told Maria abruptly, an idea striking her.

"When?" Maria wanted to know. "What am I going to say to my investors? When can I give them an answer? What are you going to do? I have a right to be kept up to date with what you are doing!"

"I'll get back to you as soon as I can," Jaylin promised, "I can't do it any sooner than that."

"All right."

Maria's voice did a switch-down from the corporate to the personal, "You're very busy these days, aren't you, Jay?"

"Aren't we all?"

"You haven't called me for such a long time."

"Maria, I talk to you nearly every day!"

"I don't mean about *work* ... "

Jaylin didn't get it.

"It was my birthday yesterday."

Jaylin got it.

"You always call me on my birthday. Are you deliberately keeping away from me because of this project?"

"Of course not!" Jaylin said with utter truthfulness. The thought hadn't occurred to her. She had completely forgotten. In a way, she was glad. Remembering Maria's birthday might have put her in a bit of a spot.

"Because I want you to know that anything that goes on between Raffles Multiplex and Stead-Semple is strictly professional and nothing to do with you and me. You know that don't you, Jay? I don't want to lose you as a friend."

It was on the tip of Jaylin's tongue to say, *isn't it a bit too late for that?* But she bit her tongue and swallowed the thought. Why was it that Maria always managed to irritate her so much? There was no reason, no reason at all, for her to be upset by what Maria said. Or was it hurt pride? After all these years?

"It's all right, Maria," Jaylin said, 'I'm sorry I missed your birthday, really. I would have called, but I've been so busy ... look, I'm sorry, but I've got a call coming in that I have to take. I'll call you back as soon as I can, OK? I've got to go now."

"Don't work too hard, Jay! Better take it easy!"

Why did even that irritate Jaylin?

"Take it easy yourself."

Jaylin took a deep breath and a can of Pepsi out of her minibar. She had just felt the stirrings of an idea. It was difficult to come up with something new for Singapore because Singapore had *everything*. Everything except chewing gum. Everything that healthy, normal, Singaporeans needed to continue functioning healthily and normally.

Jaylin told herself that what she really needed to do was think of something that Singapore was *going* to need in the near future. To anticipate a need; if possible, to create awareness of that need in people's minds and then step forward with a solution for them ... this wasn't easy. She was no sociologist. But she knew someone who was ...

Jaylin cast her mind back to the hypothesis that SuFern had presented to her:

1. *The men whom male subjugation affects most severely are heterosexual men. Women and gay men form automatic support systems but heterosexual men are on their own.*

2. *Positive 'masculine' characteristics are only celebrated when they appear in women, e.g., tough lady managers, women with a 'man's' intellect. Popular wisdom classifies 'macho' men as not very bright. All other men are categorised 'wimp'.*

3. *The pursuit of positive 'masculine' characteristics like strength, reliability and resourcefulness, are only encouraged among women and gay men.*

4. *Women and gay men have a plethora of positive role models. Heterosexual men get Jack Nicholson who fathers families he doesn't live with because he believes men have trouble functioning in a family situation.*

While all of this might be true, Jaylin didn't find it very useful or relevant. Much as she had been impressed with Dr. Lim SuFern, she was afraid that psychosociology was just one more esoteric subject of interest only to the inmates of NUS and other such institutions.

But it had *seemed* relevant enough when SuFern talked about it. It was probably the woman's excitement and enthusiasm more than anything else that had breathed life into her subject.

From her own experience, Jaylin wasn't inclined to believe in SuFern's hypothesis. After all, her grandfather seemed pretty self-assured in an alien land; her mother's boyfriend was perfectly aware he was an MCP and perfectly happy to live as one; and her father had walked out on her mother very self-righteously and got away scot-free.

No matter how Jaylin looked at it, it didn't seem to her that male subjugation was a problem for any of the men she knew, all things considered. Or, as the long-suffering wife of a passionately animal-loving friend had once said, "If that's a dog's life, I'll be a poodle!"

Jaylin smiled at the memory. The animal-loving friend was more inclined to mongrels, but the long-suffering wife had always been a Francophile – French couture, French perfumes, even French dogs, it seemed …

It is strange how our deepest-seated inclinations surface, sometimes.

"The problem," SuFern had told Jaylin, "is that the men of your generation may never develop inner standards of worth."

But then most of the women of Jaylin's generation didn't seem to have developed very credible inner standards of worth either, thought Jaylin. Maria's name was the first one to come into her mind. But her own was right there on the list too. What inner standards of worth did she have? What values did she really believe in?

She believed in pulling her own weight in the office; in keeping in lane while driving in the CTE tunnel and in flossing her teeth regularly. But did all these things add up to a worthwhile value system? It was something that Jaylin didn't want to think about.

But that was the whole point of cultivating a flourishing career, wasn't it? A flourishing, high-pressured career that would keep you too busy to ask uncomfortable questions you couldn't answer? Jaylin bent her thoughts back to the flourishing of her career.

Even if SuFern's theory of male subjugation proved true, Jaylin could not see how it lent itself to any practical application.

But she also realised that she was standing too close to the problem. Feeling as under stress as she did, she might not recognise a practical application if one came up and hit her in the face. But wasn't she also under too much time-stress to even think of taking time off for a break? Without any conscious deliberation, Jaylin picked up the receiver and tapped out Lim SuFern's office number.

"I owe you a dinner," Jaylin said when SuFern answered. It seemed natural to get straight to the point as SuFern did.

"And I'd like to pick your brains about something, if you don't mind. Would you like to come over to my Mum's place? She's having one of her free-for-all type dinner parties and she asked me to bring someone. It's the day after tomorrow, 7:30 at her place in the Delfi. People just eat and then sit around and talk. You might find it interesting ... would you like to think about it and call me back?"

"I'd love to come. What's the address of your mother's apartment?"

After SuFern accepted the invitation to dinner with flattering alacrity, Jaylin wondered if the older woman knew what she was getting herself into. But how could she, when

Jaylin herself didn't know? She had to admit that it was curiosity more than anything else that had prompted her to make the call.

Not such a very admirable trait, perhaps …

But then curiosity is probably what got us down out of trees in the first place. And then there are those who think that the world would have been a better place if we had stayed up there.

"Day after tomorrow, then."

"Day after tomorrow."

Mrs. White Had a Fright

Mrs. White
Had a fright
In the middle of the night

And so did Charlotte Goei, who woke with a start and a sudden catch in her throat as though she had only narrowly escaped something direly dreadful in a dream she could not remember. She lay still, trying to breathe normally, telling herself she was not having a heart attack.

The luminous digits of her bedside clock-radio (a Christmas present from her dear sister Constance and brother-in-law Michael) announced with bright cheeriness that it was just after three in the morning.

Charlotte felt cold, even without the air-conditioner on; even though there was sweat beading her forehead and sweat wet and slippery on her neck. The recent horror of her dream was still with her, though she could not put a face to it. She was wary of going back to sleep, in case her dream demons were lurking in wait. Instead she got up, opened her bedroom door and stood barefoot in the passageway for a moment. Her niece Stephanie's room was just across the corridor from hers.

Faint light glanced across the passage wall. A car passed on the road below, the soothing purr of its engine following it down the curve of the hill. Somewhere further off, a night bird cried.

Charlotte rested the palm of her hand lightly on Stephanie's shut door, as though by this contact she could assure herself that the girl was safely asleep in her bed. Indeed, the harmless act did calm her somewhat, and Charlotte soon returned to her own bed and sleep.

Inside her bedroom across the passageway, Stephanie lay perfectly still, as she had for so many nights now, staring at the ceiling.

At the Delphi

Margaret Chen's Orchard Delfi apartment was small, but infused throughout with an air of idiosyncratic luxury. She did not have a television in the main living room, but her hi-fi equipment was impressive and blended surprisingly well with her antique Chinese furniture. Plants thrived in lush profusion, in and around painted terracotta pots of different sizes that also housed rocks and stones of different shapes, colours and textures.

"Isn't this place neat?" Jay enthused to SuFern after introductions had been made all round. "This is the kind of apartment I want to have when I grow old myself!"

SuFern noticed that in her mother's presence, Jaylin's suave professionalism melted into gauche little girlishness. She wondered if this was conscious or unconscious; and whether it was designed to reassure the mother or the daughter ... then she caught herself and reminded herself that, for the evening at least, she was a guest.

Margaret Chen made a little *moue* at her daughter's enthusiastic use of the word 'old', then turned to smile at SuFern.

"I didn't start picking up after myself until I was forty-five; until then I prided myself on being a working woman with No Time. So now I see keeping house as more of a hobby than a responsibility. Now that I only have to please myself, I enjoy it."

It was an apartment furnished with affection, humour and great attention to detail. Family memorabilia stood side by side with graceful artifacts of small but certain value. Among the pieces, SuFern noticed a pair of cranes which may have served as an incense burner. The piece stood by itself on a wooden bracket fitted onto the wall just above eye level.

"Images of Fuxing and of Wenchang, god of literature," Margaret Chen told her guest. "To the Chinese, cranes are symbolic of happiness and also of literary elegance. Someday I'm leaving those birds to Jaylin; not that she seems to be aiming for any form of elegance from what I can see! But it may do her some good. But for now, I need them right here, for the happiness."

"You seem happy enough," SuFern ventured.

And indeed she did.

Jaylin's mother seemed, to SuFern, to have achieved an admirable balance and contentment in her life. SuFern guessed they must be about the same age. Margaret Chen could not be more than five years older than SuFern, but where SuFern was beginning to feel the approach of old age, Margaret Chen had already transcended some unseen barrier into agelessness.

Margaret Chen smiled.

"I work at it. I work hard at it, believe you me. But we can sit down and have a good gossip once I've got the dinner going. Oh, that's nice, isn't it?"

The piece that SuFern had stopped to examine was a dainty blue-white porcelain statue; a goddess holding the juyi, the precious stone of the Jade Emperor Yuhuang.

"She's standing on a lobster."

"A crayfish, Dr. Lim – "

"Please call me SuFern."

"Thank you, SuFern. Like all fish, it is an emblem of wealth, regeneration, harmony and communal bliss. She's lovely, isn't she?"

"Lovely," SuFern assented readily. Whatever she had expected of the evening, she hadn't expected a guided inspection of Chinese artifacts. But she was being charmed, in spite of herself. Charmed both by Jaylin's mother and by her own Chinese heritage that was only now beginning to stir and awaken.

In the kitchen, Chin Soon sat at the table with his sleeves folded up to his elbows and his thinning hair brushed back. He delicately peeled cooked prawns and laid them out in careful whorls on a peony patterned black porcelain plate.

While he would not take a hand in day-to-day cooking, he did not find it beneath him on company occasions to prove his contention that men were better in the kitchen when it was worth their while.

When Margaret and SuFern entered the kitchen, Jaylin was sitting on the floor, not very helpfully playing with Mei Lin. Mei Lin was her mother's black and white cat.

"Jaylin," said her mother, "since you're not doing anything useful here, come and help me fold the serviettes."

"Mother, nobody uses cloth serviettes these days, it's not hygienic."

"People who are concerned about conservation and recycling use cloth serviettes these days. Do you know how many trees are – "

"How do you want them folded, Mum?"

Mother and daughter left to tend to the serviettes.

Chin Soon looked up from his handiwork to find SuFern watching him with fascination. When he was engrossed in what he was doing, what some saw as the wealthy MCP side of him vanished.

"'There is nothing more beautiful in this world than a healthy, wise old man', Lin Yutang," he quoted.

"You like the Chinese poets?" SuFern asked.

"He says he does, but he reads them in English translations!" Margaret Chen shouted from the living room. "It doesn't count! Chin Soon, we don't have that much time. Save your poetry for when you're drinking tea under the moon!"

"Ask her about the Grey Panthers, SuFern," Chin Soon said with a sly wink. "She always has time to talk about the Grey Panthers."

"What's this about the Grey Panthers, Miss Chen?"

"Are you calling me 'Miss Chen' again, Dr. Lim?"

"Tell her, tell her."

"Are you trying to set me up again, Chin Soon?"

Set up or not, Margaret Chen was only too glad to leap into a fighting conversation. She came to stand in the kitchen doorway. The man who loved her continued stuffing prawns placidly.

"Maggie Kuhn was sixty-four in 1970 when she organized the Grey Panthers, a network of highly vocal older people around the United States who are dedicated to fighting ageism. She said that the reason why America is such a mess is because people there are too isolated from each other. The old are isolated by government policy. We could do with some action like that in Singapore!

"And while we're on the subject, Grandma Moses was seventy-eight when she began to paint in oils. And that was only because up till then she embroidered on canvas, but her fingers became too stiff to manipulate a needle. In 1960, when she was one hundred years old, she illustrated *Twas the Night before Christmas*.

"I didn't know she was so old," Jaylin said innocently, coming into the kitchen and picking a tangerine out of the carved wooden bowl on top of the microwave.

"I mean, *Twas the Night before Christmas* … "

"An edition of," her mother said primly, before turning back to SuFern, 'I'm always having to take Jaylin to task for not being precise in her language, so she loves an opportunity to get back at me a little. Come on, daughter, more serviettes await you!"

"Yo, boss."

"Isn't SuFern wonderful?" Jaylin asked her mother with shining eyes over a tray-full of water-lily serviettes.

"She's a nice woman," Margaret Chen said, "and of course I recognised her!"

"You do? Poh Poh says she gives talks, but that's not quite your kind of thing, is it?"

"Jay-Jay, I don't have one foot in the grave, you know. Isn't she the Dr. Lim SuFern who published that study, *On Female Eating Disorders?* It was a landmark study that originated in Singapore! I'm surprised that *you* haven't heard of it!"

"Why didn't you say something, then?"

"She's a guest in my house. You should never be rude to guests … Now, Jaylin, you're not going to be silly over her, are you?"

"Silly?"

"Don't pretend you don't know what I mean."

"I really don't Mom. I wanted to talk to her about something concerning a project, and you did tell me to bring a friend, so ... "

"Jaylin, I don't interfere with your life, you know that very well. But this kind of thing never works. If only you realised that sooner you wouldn't have such a hard time. For your own sake, I wish you would settle down."

"Mum, what do you want me to do? Find a man and get married? That's not going to happen, you know that's not going to happen."

"There are other sorts of relationships, you know. If you know you're not going to get married, find a good friend to live with, settle down with – find someone who you can grow old with – you can't just bury yourself in your work and expect someone to be there for you ... "

"Well ... I don't have much time to meet people these days."

"You're thirty years old, Jay."

"Thirty-one, Mother."

"Now you're making *me* feel old. I just want you to be happy, Jay. I wish you had somebody to look after you. You and your grandmother, you both refuse to make any sort of plans ... "

"I can look after myself, Mums. And you know that Poh Poh and Grandpa Celli are perfectly happy together."

"Still – a little stability is nice. It's restful for the soul. After what Maria did to you, and then that Gerry woman just getting up and disappearing like that – "

"Mum, even if I *was* interested in SuFern, she wouldn't be interested in me."

"And why not?" Motherly indignation rose to the fore.

"She's not so-inclined. Believe it or not, not all women are. Anyway, she's got a son who's older than I am!"

"So?"

"Mum, you're not trying to *encourage* me, are you?"

"Of course not. I'm just concerned about your life – "

"How are your Bali plans coming, by the way, just to change the subject?"

"Ah yes. Bali. There's something I have to talk to you about – a favour I have to ask, actually."

"You want me to cat-sit Mei Lin for you?"

"No, Mona's doing that."

"Then? Out with it, Mother. I can tell that this one's going to be a biggie!"

"Did you really grow up with so little filial piety? What can I have been thinking of?"

"Bali, probably. What's coming down, Mum?"

"Your cousin Stephanie, actually. You know her husband died?"

"No, actually I didn't."

"Well he did. Your uncle and his wife think that it would be good for Stephanie to get away from KL for a bit, come down to Singapore in other words."

"But weren't they separated already? There was some fuss about that, wasn't there? Before Aunty Constance decided it wasn't any of our business?"

"It's still a shock, you know."

"Stephanie is such a wimp! So what are we supposed to be doing with her while she's here?"

"Not 'we' Darling, I'm going to be in Bali, remember?"

"Uhmmm."

"Your grandmother says Stephanie can stay at Pasir Panjang with you until I come back. She's cleaning out the old servants' quarters behind the big house and putting her up there. It's not luxurious, but it's cosy – there's room enough and she can have some privacy there, if that's what she wants."

"You've already spoken to Poh Poh, then?"

"Well, Stephanie is her granddaughter too, you know. Your Poh Poh is concerned about Stephanie too. We all are!"

"Uhmmm. Can't she stay here with Mei Lin and you get Mona to come in and feed her every day too? If she wants privacy, this place would be a lot more private while you're away!"

"I don't think it would be good for her to be *too* alone. And Jay, if you could find the time to just talk to your cousin a little, that would be very nice ... "

"What time is she arriving, anyway?"

"Nine-thirty ... "

"Nine-thirty? Nine-thirty when?"

"Tonight, of course. Just in time for dessert. We're having lotus seeds. You must bring some back with you for your grandparents."

Fear of Flying

Once upon a time, Stephanie Lake, *nee* Chen, had loved travelling.

She had loved visiting strange and foreign places.

She had loved meeting people with different customs and different patterns of life.

She had loved getting away from the drab, safe sameness of her home life ...

Once upon a time, Stephanie Chen had loved flying. But now Stephanie hated, absolutely hated, flying. She was terrified of flying.

She had nightmares of being helplessly trapped in a plane that was plunging on its way to a fiery disaster. Just before the plane crashed, Stephanie would catch sight of her husband, dead, in the pilot's seat.

Looking for her out of his sightless eyes.

And, of course, it wasn't just in planes that she saw him.

Ever since Ralph died, Stephanie had also had nightmares of being helplessly trapped in speeding cars, of being helplessly trapped in plummeting lifts, in precariously swaying cable cars ... and each time, just before certain death, Stephanie's dead husband appeared and her wild struggles to get away from him propelled her back into consciousness.

All Stephanie's nightmare situations began with the

promise of travel, of freedom, of escape. They all ended with Stephanie trapped and helpless ... and dying with Ralph Lake.

Her sleep universe was suddenly sprung full of traps.

When she woke up, chilled and sweating in her familiar yet strange childhood bedroom, her waking universe wasn't all that much better. Sometimes she could hear her Aunt Charlotte in the next bedroom. Even at two or three in the morning, Aunt Charlotte would be moving about in her room as though she spent all night folding clothes and washing underwear. She never made much noise, just enough to let Stephanie know that she was not the only one awake in the sleeping hemisphere. Stephanie suspected that her aunt meant her companionable wakefulness as a source of comfort to Stephanie.

It wasn't.

On such restless nights, Stephanie tried to think why it was that she had married Ralph in the first place, as though this knowledge would somehow exorcise her guilt. When they first met at a friend's barbecue, Ralph had seemed so charming, so worldly, so *different* from all the other bookish, young, Malaysian-Chinese lawyers and doctors who were there that night.

Had she married Ralph only because he was *different?*

No. Stephanie had married Ralph because he had so obviously wanted to marry her. He had wooed her so enthusiastically, so boisterously, so *publicly* that it had been easier to say 'yes' than 'no'.

Turning Ralph Lake down required more energy than Stephanie Chen possessed.

Aunt Charlotte would have liked Stephanie to confide in her, to talk to her about how she felt about her marriage, her late husband, her parents, her future plans and everything else in her world of middle-class bereavement.

Stephanie didn't want to talk to her Aunt Charlotte, or anyone else, about her marriage or about Ralph Lake, either alive or dead. It wasn't that she found it too painful or that she couldn't face the thought of talking about it – it was just that she didn't have anything at all to say on the subject.

When she tried to think of something to say about her late husband, she just came up with *nothing*. And this was not Stephanie trying to put the dead man down. These days, when Stephanie tried to think of something to say about herself, she came up with the same amount of nothing. She felt as though she didn't have a self any more.

Spending her days in her parents' house didn't help. Stephanie felt as though time had passed and things had changed for everyone else but not for her. She was still her parents' only daughter, still living at home in the first bedroom on the left off the top floor landing.

And when she looked into the mirror, the same mirror that she had used during her teenage years, it was as though the mirror was empty … there was no one there at all, just an empty image that did not reflect any of the things that had been going wrong on the inside. Stephanie couldn't understand why no one around her could see that something was wrong with her. Or why they all insisted on pretending that nothing was wrong at all.

And now Stephanie was on her way to Singapore.

Stephanie didn't know why she was on her way to Singapore.

She was on her way to Singapore because her mother had driven her to Subang Airport and given her a ticket and told her to get on the plane.

Her mother had been waiting outside the departure gate to see her off. Stephanie knew that she would wait, hoping to wave goodbye to her daughter if her daughter should turn around for a final look, but Stephanie didn't turn around to look.

Aunt Charlotte had wanted to come along too. For the ride, Aunt Charlotte said, for some fresh air. Aunt Charlotte had wanted to see Stephanie safely on the plane. In fact, Aunt Charlotte would probably have been glad to go all the way to Singapore with Stephanie if only someone had suggested it. But no one had suggested it.

And at the last minute, Stephanie said to her mother, coldly, that she really couldn't stand having Aunt Charlotte come to see her off. Stephanie *knew* that Aunt Charlotte would say something meaningful and uplifting and ultimately depressing as she was leaving, and it would fragment her.

"I can't stand it, Mummy – tell Aunty Charlotte she can't come. I don't want her to come … she'll talk all the time in the car and drive me crazy. If you won't tell her then I'll just go to the airport alone by taxi."

Constance gave her daughter a strange look and went to talk to her sister. Constance drove her daughter to the airport without Charlotte. They rode in silence for most of the journey. Stephanie didn't ask her mother what she had said to Aunt Charlotte. For her part, her mother didn't say anything about Singapore or ask how long Stephanie would be staying there.

Stephanie was not going to Singapore in order to get to Singapore. Stephanie was going to Singapore to get out of Kuala Lumpur.

More than anything, Stephanie just wanted to disappear. Singapore wasn't the best place to disappear in, but Singapore was all that had offered itself, so she was taking it.

More planes crash on take-off and on landing than at any other time. This is a statistical fact.

Stephanie had read the statistics in an article on air disasters in *Reader's Digest*. Stephanie didn't see how knowing that could help anybody. If you were in an aeroplane, sooner or later you would either take off or land …

But why should she be afraid of dying in a plane crash? After all, hadn't she (during all those nights spent lying awake) thought calmly and rationally about killing herself?

The plane was taking off. Stephanie shut her eyes.

This could be her last moment alive.

Stephanie opened her eyes and looked around cautiously for an apparition of Ralph Lake. The stewardess moved to the front of the cabin and began to demonstrate safety procedures.

Stephanie told herself: *this stewardess has done the shuttle flight from Kuala Lumpur to Singapore a hundred times and has never been in a plane that crashed.*

Stephanie realised: *this* is *really pushing the odds.*

As far as she knew, no plane had crashed while travelling from Kuala Lumpur to Singapore.

It sounds like something is *really overdue to happen.*

But hadn't there been that plane (in 1982? or had it been

1983?) that had crash-landed between Singapore and Kuala Lumpur?

The engines ground up into a steady rumble and the plane eased into a forward movement.

If Stephanie remembered correctly, there had been no fatalities that time. It had been an MAS flight and the pilot had landed the plane safely just outside Subang.

The stewardess smiled at her and handed her a tray with a bun and a cup on it.

"Orange juice? Pineapple juice?"

Stephanie wondered if their pilot was the one who had landed the plane safely just outside Subang. Stephanie wondered if their pilot had a drinking problem or whether he had had a fight with his wife the night before.

The plane stopped taxiing and paused as though to draw a deep breath and gird its loins.

This could be my last moment alive, I should have taken the train. Or just stayed in Kuala Lumpur. I wonder if it's too late to jump up and say I have to get off the plane? Later on, after the crash they'll say I was psychic or something ... or that I planted the bomb ...

Of course Stephanie was too self-conscious to do anything so embarrassing.

As though in response to her thoughts, the low hum built into a roar and then the scream of charging machinery. A lurch forward, sudden acceleration, and they were airborne. Stephanie braced herself for the impact that would come when they ran smack into another jet, but it didn't come.

They were free of the earth.

The strange thing was, Stephanie reflected, that even if you felt that you had nothing to live for, you still didn't want to die. At least not by accident, totally meaninglessly.

Like the way Ralph had died.

After Dinner

Jaylin capitulated, as both she and her mother had known all along she would.

"All right, you win," Jaylin told her mother just minutes before Stephanie rang the doorbell of Margaret Chen's apartment.

"All right. I'll keep an eye on poor old Stephanie. You've already told Poh Poh and Grandpa Rob that she's going to be arriving tonight, have you?"

"I mentioned it to them, yes, subject to you agreeing to keep an eye on her, of course."

Margaret Chen fussed delicately with a leaf of fern that wasn't standing *quite* right in its planter. She was very adept at playing the part of an absent-minded, middle-aged mother when she thought the situation called for it.

"Robert said that it was really up to *you,* since the two of them just about manage to keep themselves going, and any extra work to do with Stephanie coming down would fall to you … I keep telling them, they should think about selling that enormous old place and getting something easier to manage – and a maid to help with things. But Robert says it's entirely up to Ma, and you know how your Poh Poh is about having strangers living in her house … I wish there was some way I could persuade them to have someone in to look after the house. Or just come in a few times a week to help. It's not as though they can't afford it, but Robert just says it's up to your Poh Poh, so what to do?"

"Grandpa Celli washes his hands more often than Pontius Pilate. Stephanie's only here temporarily, right? This is not going to be a permanent … "

"Of course not," said her mother soothingly. "Would I do something like that to you?"

Jaylin gave her progenitress a dark look but said nothing.

"Do you always get your way?" SuFern asked Margaret Chen later.

"Only when it's something that matters enough!"

Margaret gave SuFern a searching look.

SuFern felt as though she was being assessed, as in *Can she be trusted? What does she want?*

Then the older woman smiled, immediately dispelling that impression.

"When you love someone very much, you want the best for them. And you try to bring it about, fair means or foul … and whether they like it or not!"

"Your niece Stephanie needs – " began SuFern knowingly.

"No. My daughter, Jaylin. Doing good to someone else does you more good in the long run than having good done to you. I learnt that the hard way. Jay's my daughter and I want to make it easier for her if I can. And of course you're right. Stephanie has her problems, too. But it's so much more difficult to reach Stephanie. She's so closed in, poor child. It's all the fault of that blessed mother of hers!"

SuFern and Jaylin's mother were standing in the tiny Delfi kitchen waiting for their after-dinner coffee to percolate. SuFern had heard something of Stephanie's sad story while helping to scrape and rinse their dinner plates in the kitchen.

"What do you think Jaylin can do for Stephanie, then? She's very busy, you know ... with her work and everything ... "

"I don't think she has to *do* anything, just get to know her a little. They are cousins, after all!

Margaret handed SuFern a tray of coffee paraphernalia.

"Here, just put this beside Chin Soon, will you? Thank you."

Their conversation was over.

SuFern found Jaylin alone on the glassed-in balcony amidst a jungle of potted plants, looking down on the brightly-lit hustle and bustle of Orchard Road. Jaylin was deep in thought, but surfaced when SuFern came to stand quietly beside her.

"How's it going?"

"Terrific," Jaylin rolled her eyes. "I don't remember the last time I had such a wild, rollicking time!"

"Your cousin's pretty quiet, isn't she?"

Jaylin turned to eye Stephanie who was mooning on the sofa looking politely bored out of her skull.

"She's just shy," Jaylin said.

No, Stephanie wasn't, SuFern decided. Stephanie was not being shy. SuFern couldn't tell why, but she sensed Stephanie was being hostile; hostile and reserved like a beautiful cat. *Keep your distance,* her demeanour said; *if provoked, I hiss and I scratch.*

After a few, foiled attempts to draw her into conversation, the other guests had fallen back on the simple resort of treating her as a pretty but backward child and smiling at her now and then while they made conversation around her. Stephanie was sitting on the edge of a sofa that Margaret had draped with a Mexican shawl, next to a miniature palm tree in a blue Mexican pot.

The plant looked more animated than Stephanie did. And it was painted plaster.

"I guess we should go in and make talk," Jaylin said finally.

"I know. Thank you, by the way."

"What for?"

"For inviting me here tonight. Your mother is wonderful. I'm glad I met her. I've never met anyone quite like her before!"

"I don't think *anyone* has," Jaylin said, with just a touch of grimness.

Inside the apartment, the telephone rang.

"For you, Jaylin," Chin Soon called, a note of surprise in his voice, "Robert Celli."

Jaylin went to the phone, a little crease of anxiety appearing between her eyes. Being Jaylin, her mind immediately leapt to the worst possible reasons that could have made her step-grandfather call.

Not Poh Poh, please ... nothing's happened to my Poh Poh ...

"Chocky isn't very well. Your grandmother's very worried. She gave her some Panadol about two hours ago, but the cat seems worse – do you know where the 24-hour veterinary hospital is? The cat looks very bad, she's lying still, not moving."

Jaylin started to give directions to Mount Pleasant, her mind wondering if it would be faster for her to return home for the cat.

"Never mind the hospital," SuFern said, when she heard what the situation was.

"Tell your grandparents to stay put at home. I'll call my son. Can you give me your home address? He's the best vet in Singapore when you can get him away from his aikido. He'll be able to tell you if your cat needs hospitalization and if anything needs to be done immediately he can take care of it there and then. Write the address down for me – may I use your phone? He'll meet us there – "

"Such a bother for him," Margaret Chen murmured.

"Steve will do anything for animals," said Steve's mother with absolute certainty.

Strangers in the Night

Chocky was lying motionless on her side when Jaylin, followed by SuFern and, more slowly, by Stephanie, ran into the house.

Chocky was not dead. Yet. But you had to look twice to be sure the tiny limp body was still breathing.

She stirred when Jaylin stroked her, and looked imploringly at her out of the mute eyes of a suffering animal, but she was too weak to mew.

Poh Poh Celli looked, if anything, even worse stricken.

Stephanie walked out of the house, down the porch steps to the driveway and vomited, quietly and politely, into the drain beside it.

The only other sounds came from the voices in the house and the crickets in the dark. The smell of rain was in the air, carried intoxicatingly high on the wind that blew in over the sea and brought with it the tang of salt and the boom of tankers anchored in deep waters.

Steve Thurairatnam's car pulled up behind Jaylin's before Stephanie had time to go back up into the house. She stood back in the shadows and said nothing. Steve glanced at her, then caught sight of his mother who had come out on to the porch. He headed towards her. Steve Thurairatnam was a broad-shouldered, bespectacled man with the strong, quiet air of a Chinese-Indian Clark Kent.

"What's wrong with her? Can you help her?" Poh Poh Celli asked with a tremor in her voice.

Steve, examining the cat's eyes and the lining of its mouth, said nothing. He would answer her when he had something to say. But when he stood up, he rested his hand for a moment on the old woman's shoulder as though she was a nervous animal that needed soothing.

Jaylin began to cry. She was very angry with herself and at the same time she didn't care whether she was angry or not. She hadn't cried since her father left. Not even when Gerry had walked out on her. Tears ran out of her eyes and out of her nose and she hated her feeling of helplessness.

"Hey," said Steve quite kindly, "the cat's not dead yet, but she will be if we don't get a move on. We have to get her in fast. What do you carry her in, normally?"

Jaylin's grandmother brought a box lined with Chocky's towels and Steve put the puffy-faced cat inside, quickly but gently.

What Jaylin really hated was having to stand by helplessly, not knowing what to do. What good was it to be strong, successful, secure ... if you couldn't do a thing for the dumb animal who loved you and trusted you to look after her?

And when was the last time I took the time to play with her, anyway?

There was something about Steve that inspired confidence and confidences, Jaylin thought. If only he was a woman she could have fallen for him. Why had she never thought of dating a vet?

Outside, Stephanie had emptied out her guts, so she felt

relatively safe for the time being. Her reaction to stress was putting a whole new slant on bulimia.

"What's going to happen to her? Is she going to be all right?"

"But what happened ... did she eat something wrong, was it some kind of infection? What happened to her?"

Steve answered Jaylin without stopping as he strode purposefully out of the house carrying Chocky's box.

"I think your cat was poisoned."

"Poisoned! But who would do – no, that's not possible ..."

"Paracetamol poisoning."

"Paracetamol as in Panadol?"

"Exactly as in Panadol. Good intentions may be killing your cat ... is your friend all right?"

Stephanie was leaning against a pillar and staring blankly at the ground in front of her.

"I don't believe we've met?" Steve said, walking over to stand in front of her. He planted his shoes in the patch of earth her eyes had been focused on. His voice was low and soothing, geared to soothe a nervous or frightened animal.

Good shoes, Stephanie thought. But worn.

"My name is Steve Thurairatnam."

Stephanie looked up from his shoes to his face, but did not speak.

Even in her distraction, Jaylin noticed that Stephanie had never looked more fragilely, more luminously lovely. Even the pale green tint to her complexion seemed to suit her.

The vet in Steve could not turn away from a living thing so obviously in a distressed condition. If she had been four-footed and furry, Steve would have picked her up and taken responsibility for her care, feeding and medical needs there and then.

But as she was not, he did not.

Not immediately.

Introducing the Late Ralph Lake

Introducing Ralph Lake, the late husband of Stephanie Chen, is something that should really have been done *before* his unfortunate demise. Failing that, he will be introduced now, as background to our understanding of his wife.

After all, it's better to be introduced late than never.

Once upon a time, Ralph Emerson Lake had been the bright and promising only son of a teacher and his homemaker wife who lived on 33rd Street in Bayonne, New Jersey, 07002, U.S.A.

When little Ralphie was eleven years old, he won a statewide spelling bee and ironed his own shirts to spare his mother the effort. Mrs. Ruth Lake thought her son was a miracle, a genius, and heaven-sent as compensation for her mild, unambitious husband. Her boy would become a lawyer, or a doctor, even.

Anyway, he would be rich.

She *knew* that as surely as the Virgin Mary knew she was going to bear the Lord's child – even though Ruth Lake was Jewish and really more of an Elizabeth. After all, by the time Little Ralphie came along, the Lakes had long resigned themselves to childlessness.

Little Ralphie would go far. And he meant to. He set his sights on New York first.

Bayonne, New Jersey, is not far from New York City in geographic terms, but in reality it exists in a different dimension. Imagine if you can, the difference between Kuala Kangsar and Kuala Lumpur ... multiplied a hundred times. America is a large country, and especially large are the gulfs that separate the American people from each other.

Ralph Lake wanted to make it big in the big city. But he had certain obstacles to surmount first.

Nature had not been kind to Ralph Lake. Nature gave Ralph Lake a mother who insisted on cutting his hair (as well as his father's) at home because she had once spent 25 dollars on a hair-dressing course. Ruth Lake didn't see why she should pay someone else to do something she could do at home for free.

Nature also gave Ralph Lake a short father. In America, it is a serious social handicap to be less than 5' 6", especially if you are a White Man.

Ralph married his college sweetheart, Karen Auer (5' 3").

But Karen wasn't as adaptable as Ralph, and she didn't share his vision of what Ralph could do with Ralph's life. She wanted to settle down and have a family. She wanted to buy a pair of hair-dressing scissors and cut her Ralph's hair at home.

So Ralph Lake ran away from his wife. Anyway, his mother had never liked Karen.

Ralph ran to South America and tried to set up a tour agency that was to specialise in trotting rich college kids around the globe (i.e. to South America). After getting his divorce from Karen, he married Antonia Lopez. This marriage lasted till he and Antonia went back to live in New York, the tour agency having failed to live up to his expectations.

Antonia was instantly at home in the city, so much so

that Ralph felt like an outsider by comparison. He accused Antonia of only having married him to get her Green Card. Antonia snapped back, "I didn't – if I had thought of it I would have chosen a man better-looking!".

To complicate matters, she became pregnant. Sharp tongued or not, Ralph had always found her very compatible in bed. He always used condoms for sex, so naturally he accused her of having been unfaithful. Ralph didn't really believe his wife had been unfaithful, but being a father would cramp his style. Antonia agreed to an abortion. Antonia wanted a family desperately and she believed abortion equalled murder, but she thought if she made Ralph happy this time, he would settle down and be normal.

Ralph felt so bad about this that he left her a note and jumped ship on the day that she went for the abortion that he had insisted on. He called her, once, to say he was back in New York.

She replied, "I am going to kill you. You made me kill my baby."

Ralph hung up. Women were really so unreasonable and vindictive.

This time he ran all the way to Australia. He waited in Australia until his divorce came through. Australia was a lot more welcoming in the pre-Depression days. Ralph thought that with all the experience he had as an American he wouldn't have any problem making it Big in Australia.

He made it Medium.

But American PR and self-promotion still pay off in the ex-colonies. So from America, Ralph Lake moved on to Malaysia and Singapore. And there he met and married Stephanie Chen.

To his credit, Ralph Lake had been in love with Stephanie Chen. To him, she seemed all sweet, unwoken, wealthy innocence ... just what the would-be doctor had ordered. Once he had decided that they were meant for each other, he had gone all out and wooed and won her in a whirlwind courtship that succeeded within months of their first meeting. It had been a sad, strange little wedding, full of expensively dressed people afraid of saying the wrong thing. The Chens gave their only daughter and her husband an apartment to begin their married life in.

And now Ralph Lake was dead.

I Get No Kick From This Pain ...

I get no kick from this pain,
And no business call can thrill me at all
Consultancy' s just such a bore
When you've got a drip in your paw ...

It started out as one of Jaylin's worst days at work ever.

In the early hours of the morning, after Steve had done what he could to make Chocky comfortable, he shooed everyone out of the veterinary surgery and made them all go home. To her surprise, Jaylin had fallen asleep almost immediately. But her dreams were so full of visions of cats in distress that when her radio alarm hauled her out of her disturbed sleep at 6:30 it had come as a relief.

Poh Poh, red-eyed, was already in the kitchen. She told Jaylin (again) that she had not given anything to the cat that could have made her sick. Jaylin told her (again) that she knew she hadn't meant to.

Her barely concealed impatience with her grandmother suddenly cracked to reveal her own fear beneath. She suddenly saw her Poh Poh as an old woman for the first time, and it frightened her. Her grandmother stood in the kitchen in a limp, faded, floral housecoat looking old and frail. Jaylin could not bear it nor could she think of anything to say to comfort the grieving woman.

"I have to be in at work early today."

Poh Poh's old. She might die soon. How would you like it if those were the last words you ever spoke to her?

Before leaving the house, Jaylin went into her grandmother's room and gave her a quick hug.

"Chocky's going to be fine," she said. But she was expressing hope rather than reassurance.

Jaylin stopped by the vet surgery to look in on her cat before work. The clinic wasn't open yet, but Steve's assistant let her in and brought her round to the small room at the back where Chocky was. In the bright light of day, the clinic wasn't the terrifying place it had seemed the night before. Instead, it looked drab and somehow pathetic.

Jaylin knew that Chocky wouldn't like the strange smells ... frightened animal smells overlaid with disinfectant. She was 'stable', lying limply in what looked like a padded fish tank with a needle taped to her paw and a drip suspended above her.

If Jaylin had been a lesser mortal, she would have called in sick and let Stead-Semple sort things out the best they could without her. If she had been a mother with sick children she would have called in sick and no one would have thought worse of her for that. But she was not a mother with sick children. A mother with sick children could not have risen to where Jaylin was with Stead-Semple.

Jaylin was just a woman with a poisoned cat, an old grandmother, a cousin going through a break-down and a Pepsi addiction.

If she gets better, I'll play with her more. I'll clean her litter more often. I'll bathe her religiously once a month.

Part of Jaylin knew she was not going to be able to stick to her good resolutions when gratitude receded with time. But cats, like saints, are forgiving (though occasionally aloof) creatures.

Jaylin had been staring at the screen of her computer but she hadn't read a word on it.

She reached for the telephone. Again.

"This is Lee Jaylin. Can you tell me how my cat is?"

The nurse-receptionist at the veterinary clinic was a patient woman.

"No change from the last time you called, Miss Lee. Still sleeping."

The last time she called had been less than 10 minutes ago. A human nurse would have been less patient. Perhaps dealing with animals makes people better tempered …

"Raffles Multiplex," said Mun Ee at the door. She had been fielding calls all morning. "Very urgent, she said. It's Maria Gong on the line and she sounds very upset about something."

"All right. I'll take it. Thanks."

Concern was written all over Mun Ee's round, maternal face as she shut the door behind her. Jaylin hadn't told her what – or indeed that anything – was wrong, but Mun Ee's radar was super-sensitively calibrated by years of experience. Besides, Jaylin had received more personal calls that morning than she normally got in a week. Even Chin Soon had called, from the airport, to see if there was any improvement in the cat's condition.

Mona-who-lived-above-her-mother's-shop had called to tell Jaylin that the cat would recover if she was meant to recover and that even if she didn't, all good cats were rewarded in heaven. Someone had seen a vision where heaven was full of animals.

This probably should have made Jaylin feel better, but somehow it didn't.

Would her pussycat ever forgive her?

Chocky had originally belonged to Jaylin and Gerry. They had found her as a tiny kitten in a hawker centre, mewing pathetically in a drain. But both Gerry and Jaylin were clocking up exhausting hours at work and, even before Gerry had taken off for the unknown, Poh Poh Celli had gradually taken over Chocky's care and feeding. Though she knew her grandmother loved the cat, Jaylin felt that she had abandoned the tiny animal and was somehow responsible for what had happened.

And Jaylin realized that she deeply resented the fact that Gerry was not around to feel guilty too.

Maria's voice on the phone hauled her back to harsh reality.

"Lee Jaylin. What the hell are you playing at, I'd like to know?"

Jaylin wondered for an instant how on earth she could ever have been in love with this woman. Had Maria always had such a strident voice? Maria was not trying to be belligerent. She thought her slashing assault was witty and vivacious.

"Well? I'd like to know what you've got to say for yourself!"

"What is it, Maria?" Jaylin said tiredly.

"The draft proposal that you sent me. You're not *serious* about this, are you?"

"Why not?"

"Retirement apartments? We're looking at a sophisticated,

up-market, glam lifestyle complex and you're talking about old people in wheelchairs? Please, come on!"

"Sophisticated, up-market, glamorous people get old too, you know. If they're lucky. This will be a way for people to relax and enjoy some of the things that they've worked all their lives to achieve. We won't call them *retirement apartments,* of course. This will be about growing old in a sophisticated, up-market, glamorous way. Everybody there will be looked after like an aging Gloria Swanson or a retired Winston Churchill. Children will be jealous but nobody under fifty is allowed to move in unless *married* to somebody over fifty. It will be a treat for grandchildren to visit grandma and grandpa ... Sweetie, growing old is about to become a privilege that overworked youngies like you and me will look forward to!"

Jaylin had already said as much on paper – Maria obviously preferred the personal delivery.

"You're really serious about this!" Maria said.

Maria liked the idea, she was already sold on it, Jaylin could tell. But Maria Fernandez Gong was not in the habit of saying 'I like it!' Maria never missed a chance to attack first, just in case something else could be squeezed out of the deal. She always needed someone else to put the first penny in the pot.

Jaylin once believed that the miracle of the loaves and fishes had been brought about by a few hundred Marias, each with a couple of loaves and a fish or two hidden under her cloak and not wanting to bring it out (in case she had to *share* with the less foresighted) until shamed into fellowship by the small boy. So small boys served a purpose in the overall scheme of things too ...

"Yes, I'm really serious," Jaylin said steadily. "Have I *ever* sent you a proposal that I wasn't really serious about?"

"No ... I mean ... "Maria was rapidly switching into her gushy-enthusiastic mode, "it's just that this is such a totally different concept ... I don't know if people will be ready for it."

"If people were ready, somebody else would have come up with it. The secret is to come up with something *just* before people are ready; kick them into the next phase. They'll thank you after you've done it. After living in Singapore for so many years, you should be familiar with the concept?"

"Hmmm," said Maria. She was thinking. If the truth be told, she preferred to pick up ideas just *after* someone else had come up with them and found them viable. Then she could move in and improve on a tried and tested formula.

Jaylin was heartily sick of the whole business.

"If you don't like it, fine, don't use it. Find somebody else to work this with you. But if you steal this one, Maria, I'm going to sue the panties off you, I'm warning you now."

Jaylin's tone was calm and friendly, even warm. She had gone beyond exasperation. She smiled into the phone, for total effect.

"Did I say I didn't like the idea?" bleated Maria, back-pedalling fast, "I *like* the idea. I like it very much! That's why I'm so concerned that it doesn't get shot down before it gets a fair *chance* ... not everybody can see things the way you and I do!"

Maria's back-pedalling was practised and graceful.

"It's just that I had to know whether you were going to stand by it before I went all out to push for it ... you know what it's like here. Everybody has an idea but they all expect somebody else to do the work while they sit back and get the credit for coming up with it. Whereas you and I know that 90 percent of the time, the concept doesn't count for anything until you get to the stage where you're refining ... "

Yes, quite, yes. Jaylin knew all this by heart. She had used the line often enough herself.

"Just a minute, Maria. I've got another call coming through – "

She put Maria on hold for 30 seconds and took a swig out of her can of Pepsi.

''I'm sorry, something's come up – "she lied with the panache of long experience, "I'm sorry, but I've really got to take this one. Outstation call ... "

"Right. So I'm going to go ahead and present this to our clients just as it is. Good work, Jay. Thanks for coming in on this one!"

Jaylin didn't find Maria's complete turnaround strange. For Maria, getting worked up about things was all part of the job. Jaylin was used to that. Once upon a time she had found it fascinating. Gerry said it was all an unnecessary expenditure of energy. But Gerry had always had a bit of a bee in her bonnet about Maria. Unnecessarily, of course. But Jaylin hadn't minded.

But then what good was Gerry herself? Gerry wasn't even around. Gerry had said that she loved Chocky, but if Chocky had died, Gerry wouldn't have known or cared. Well, perhaps *not cared* was a bit strong. But if she didn't know, she couldn't care, could she?

For the first time, Jaylin acknowledged how much she resented, truly and absolutely *resented* Gerry taking off into the unknown the way she had. For leaving Jaylin to face a sick cat and all the other (the many other) problems of life on her own.

True, Lim SuFern had been most helpful ... for a woman with an adult son who was a veterinarian.

A Sign

A sign was what Stephanie Chen needed.

Alone in her grandmother's house, Stephanie Chen was fast discovering that being alone and unhappy in Singapore was much the same as being alone and unhappy in Kuala Lumpur. Indeed, as only too many people know only too well, being alone and unhappy feels much the same any place on the surface of this planet.

Stephanie had no pressing needs. She had no immediate grievances. She was not homeless, starving, abused or politically discriminated against. Many people were much worse off than she was, but being aware of this didn't make her feel any better about herself. Think about it. How do you suppose the fat woman at the buffet table feels when you ladle more char kway teow onto her plate and say, "Don't let it go to waste! Think of all the starving children in Somalia!"

Stephanie was not grieving over her estranged husband's death.

I can't feel sorry that he's dead. I would rather he wasn't, but I can't feel that it has anything to do with me. No, that's a lie. I do feel something. I am glad that Ralph is dead. I am glad that he is dead and I should not try to pretend that I am sorry. But I wish that he didn't die like that. I wish that he just disappeared. I wish that I had never married him. I wish that I had never met him.

Stephanie fumbled a tissue out of the packet and blew her nose.

If we had never met, I could have gone on with my life and he would have gone on with his life and he would not be dead now and I would not be guilty.

Stephanie knew that she was not to blame for Ralph's death. But while she accepted this intellectually, she had trouble believing it emotionally. The body demanded some kind of penance before it dared to believe in absolution.

That was why Stephanie needed a sign.

She needed something that came from outside of herself. Something that would move her out of herself, out of the limbo that she was in.

If there's a God – I need a sign …

At that instant, the telephone rang. The thought that struck Stephanie immediately was that it was Ralph on the other end of the line. She froze. The telephone rang again. And again. Unable to help herself, she picked up the receiver, steeling herself to hear Ralph's high-pitched giggle.

"Stephanie Chen?" said a calm, low voice, "this is Steve Thurairatnam, the vet. We met the other night at your grandmother's house."

Stephanie hung on to her end of the line, as though her life depended on it. Was this her sign?

"Yes?"

"Stephanie, I was hoping you would agree to come to Indonesia with me."

Leaving on a Jet Plane

"Stephanie said what?"

Mrs. Constance Chen could only repeat what she had just said, "She said that she was going to Indonesia on a holiday ... "

"That's not *all* she said!" Constance's sister almost screamed at her. "She said that she was going with some strange man!"

"He must be somebody she knows or she wouldn't be going with him just like that, I suppose," Constance Chen said, trying to remain reasonable as her elder sister ranted over the dining table.

Of course the news had come as a shock to Constance. It had come as a shock to them all that Stephanie had suddenly taken it into her head to go to Indonesia ...

But ... Stephanie had sounded so much more awake, so much more *alive* than she had in a long time. Constance just wanted her vibrant, alive little girl back again.

"You never *think*!" Charlotte ranted at her married sister. "You could have let me know as soon as Stephanie phoned, you could have called me to the phone and I could have spoken to her, why didn't you? You don't think of me or my feelings at all, you are a cold and heartless woman with no idea at all what it is to be a mother!"

Michael Chen stepped in at this point. He did not care to have his wife being spoken to in this manner, even if the speaker was her own sister who had lived with them since their marriage.

"None of us expected Stephanie to go off like that. But we agreed that she needed to get away for a while ... so she's getting away. If she's found a friend to go with her, so much the better! You must remember that Stephanie is not a child any more. She's an adult and a married woman who can make decisions for herself!"

Charlotte Goei stared at her brother-in-law with unconcealed dislike in her eyes. She sat quietly till he had finished speaking, then she rose to her feet and left the table.

"Where are you going, Charlotte?" Constance cried out.

At the same time as her husband said, "Let her go – "

If the man had not spoken, Charlotte would probably have ignored her sister's protest. But since he did, she spoke, so as not to let him have the last word. 'I'm going to the airport. I'm going to Singapore. I pray to God that I can get there in time to talk some sense into that silly girl. If necessary I will go to Indonesia and bring her home. You – " looking at Michael Chen, " – see where all your liberal ideas have led to?"

"My liberal ideas?"

"But Charlotte ... shall I come with you?" Constance said, confused as to where her dignity and duty lay. "What should I do?"

"What you do is of no concern to me. I am going to bring my daughter home."

Indonesia with Steve

Indonesia with Steve offered Stephanie escape from the rut she had been in.

But on the other hand, a rut can be a fine and protected place. Stephanie wasn't sure whether she was embarking on a journey of self-preservation or self-destruction. Stephanie didn't know if this man (who had, remembering his name, once sexually propositioned her husband) had come to save her or destroy her.

But whatever his motivation, Steve Thurairatnam had called to her like her own personal nemesis, and it had not occurred to her to turn down his invitation.

At Changi Airport Terminal 2, Stephanie saw Steve coming towards her with a knapsack on his back.

Stephanie was wheeling one large suitcase and balancing a soft carry-on bag and a make-up case on top of it. She wondered if Steve was going to be embarrassed about being seen with her and all her travel paraphernalia.

Stephanie had also arrived half an hour later than Steve had asked her to. She wondered if Steve was going to make a fuss about her lack of punctuality. Stephanie decided that if Steve made the least fuss about anything, she was going to turn around and catch a taxi right back to Pasir Panjang

Road. Or better still, right back to Malaysia. But that really wouldn't be better at all, would it?

With the state that her mind was in, Stephanie could only take reality in very small, carefully demarcated doses.

Steve didn't look at all upset or reproachful. Steve looked delighted to see Stephanie again.

"She's here!" he called to someone over his shoulder as he walked towards her and took her trolley from her. Stephanie realised that Steve had been afraid that she would change her mind at the last minute and not turn up. Stephanie wondered what it was like to feel so much enthusiasm about *anything*.

A young girl bounced up to Stephanie, right behind Steve, "Hello, you must be Stephanie! My name is Annie, I'm your tour guide – "

Stephanie let herself be taken in hand. It was good to be seen as a unit with a man again, a man who automatically took responsibility for you and your luggage and could work out where you were supposed to go and what you were supposed to do, and only laughed when you said that you'd forgotten to change *any* Indonesian money for the trip ... because he had brought more than enough rupiahs for you both.

Stephanie missed being looked after by a man. Women could be very friendly and supportive when you were down, but they expected you to be properly appreciative and *aware* of their consideration all the time. Men, even gay men like Steve, were much better at making a girl feel good about herself.

Stephanie could feel herself relaxing into the trip. Stephanie could feel herself relaxing into the way people glanced at her and Steve and accepted them as a couple. Stephanie knew that they made a good-looking couple.

A little bat squeak deep inside Stephanie said, *if only,* but Stephanie quashed it.

After all, Steve Thurairatnam wasn't just gay ... Steve Thurairatnam was a *vet.*

Stephanie was so relaxed, in fact, that she forgot to psyche herself into not noticing the plane taking off.

At the first sickening lurch upwards, Stephanie blanched.

Steve didn't seem to notice. He was looking out of the window. He turned and grabbed Stephanie's hand. *Can't you see I'm frozen in a state of panic hysteria?* Stephanie wanted to scream at Steve, but she was too frozen to scream.

"Look, look at the sails on the water!" said Steve. "Isn't it a beautiful sight? When we get back from Indonesia we must go sailing. Don't you love sailing?"

Stephanie was looking in spite of herself.

The sails were tiny, white and carefree on the silver dancing sea.

Stephanie decided, right there and then, that she loved sailing too. It was a love that would bless her for the rest of her life.

Stephanie had wondered, a little, whether a vet would be able to come up with enough conversation to make him good company for a woman with no conversation at all.

"Have you seen Koch's *The Year of Living Dangerously?*" Steve asked.

"No – "

"The lobby bar that the foreign journalists used to hang out in, it's gone now but it used to be in the HI."

"The Ha-ee?"

"Hotel Indonesia. On Jalan MH Thamrin. It's still got

great atmosphere, you should see the Ramayana Terrace ... bizarre and wonderful. If the tour is a disaster, or you get sick of it at any time, just say so and we'll check in at the HI and stay there till we go back to Singapore, OK?"

"OK. You know, Steve – "

"Hmmm?"

"Right now I don't know if I ever want to go back to Singapore again!"

When their plane arrived at the Sukarno-Hatta Airport, Stephanie was so absorbed in their discussion of crab-eating macaques, hornbills, green turtles and civet cats that she didn't even notice the bump and she forgot to be alarmed over her statistical chance of surviving.

Stephanie was beginning a trip out of herself.

Jakarta was a hot, crowded blur. The tour bus wove laboriously through traffic, but Stephanie felt very detached and above it all. Their tour guide was giving them information about the city they were passing through, but Stephanie was happier dreaming out of the window.

Now and then Steve looked across to her and she smiled.

Close to someone who made no demands on her, and detached from her immediate surroundings, she knew now that was how she was happiest. Stephanie didn't give a thought to what was happening back in Malaysia or in Singapore. In fact she shut it all resolutely from her mind because she wanted to put it all behind her.

Yet there was somehow some *rightness* in the fact that she was travelling with a man who had once propositioned, and been rejected by, her late and unlamented husband.

When Will I See You Again?

Chin Soon was not a happy man when a crisis at work made it impossible for *him* to leave Singapore after he had persuaded *her* to take time out in Bali with him.

Margaret took it well, of course, she always did. In fact she took it so well that it made him wonder whether she had really wanted to go with him, or whether she had agreed to the trip simply to please him. However, the thought that she might have agreed to something to please him did not displease him, so *that* was not the reason why Chin Soon was not a happy man.

The crisis was dealt with (such incompetent subordinates these days!) and since they had both cleared their schedules, they had some free time to spend together.

"We don't have to tell anyone that we didn't go!" Margaret said. "This will be better than taking a trip, because we won't even have to travel to get away!"

This was a pleasant prospect, though Chin Soon was still a touch disappointed over Bali – and he couldn't even take it out on Margaret since it hadn't been her fault they hadn't gone.

What *really* upset Chin Soon was that just as they were settling down nicely in her apartment, her door bell rang. It rang loudly, insistently, and repeatedly. Whoever was there was not taking no for answer.

"I thought you told everybody that you were going to be away?"

"I did," Margaret said, looking perplexed. She was a very organized woman who did not usually slip up on details like most women in Chin Soon's experience.

The door bell rang again. Even more insistently.

"Well, somebody doesn't know that you're supposed to be away," he pointed out.

"Maybe it's the newspaper man collecting money or something," she said, beginning to get up.

"No ... don't answer, they'll go away, whoever they are. "

He was an orderly man who didn't like his plans being upset.

The doorbell rang again. A really prolonged peal.

"Maybe they're burglars," Margaret suggested mischievously, "making sure that there's no one home before they break in and burgle the place?"

This upset him. Chin Soon didn't like burglars and violence, even in jokes. Margaret should have been aware of that, and it wasn't very considerate of her to upset him. Since he wasn't very pleased with her, he let her go to the door alone and find out who was ringing the door bell with such persistence.

It was a woman.

She was a woman whom neither of them recognised. At least, neither of them recognised her immediately.

"Yes?" said Margaret Chen politely.

"I am looking for Stephanie," the woman said firmly. She looked suspiciously over Margaret's shoulder, as though she expected to find Stephanie skulking behind a piece of living-room furniture. If so, she was disappointed, because the only person there was Chin Soon.

"Stephanie's gone on a short holiday to central and western Java," Margaret said helpfully. "She made her plans in a bit of a hurry ... she should be back next week. Perhaps you would like to leave a number where she can reach you, Mrs. – er?"

"I am Stephanie's mother," said Charlotte Goei, every stout fibre of her trembling with all the long-suppressed emotions of motherhood.

"No, you're not," said Margaret Chen firmly.

She wasn't at all close to her sister-in-law Constance, but she was sure that she would have been able to pick out Constance in a crowd, let alone standing in front of her front door and ringing her door bell insistently. For one thing, Constance was a great deal thinner. But this woman did have the look of Constance about her. She looked like an older, stouter, more disappointed model of Michael Chen's wife.

"What is the matter?" asked Chin Soon, in the bored, capable voice of a man who is coming to help untangle the sort of fuss and bother that irrational women are always getting themselves knotted up in.

"This ... this woman ... " Margaret wondered whether the strange woman was insane and dangerous. She didn't seem to be dangerous, but these days it can be so difficult to tell if someone is about to pull a chopper on you, or try to throw you off your balcony.

"Who are you? How can we help you?" Chin Soon edged his way in front of Margaret.

"My name is Charlotte Goei," the woman began. Then she stopped, looking uncomfortably at Chin Soon, because Chin Soon was staring at her, his mouth hanging shamelessly agape ...

"What is it?" Margaret Chen cried in a panic, "Chin Soon! Chin Soon! What's wrong?"

Margaret's first thought was that the strange woman had stabbed Chin Soon with a barbecue skewer. You read about such things being done, and how they were instantly fatal.

"Chin Soon?" said the woman, now gaping as shamelessly at Chin Soon as Chin Soon was gaping at her. "Chin Soon …"

"I've already told you," Margaret said to the woman, "Stephanie is not here. If you want to leave a number where she can reach you, you're welcome to. But I think you'd better go now. I don't know who you are or what you want from her, but I do know one thing. You are certainly not Stephanie's mother!"

"But I am!" the woman said, her words coming slowly out of her hanging jaw that did not close.

"And he, Chin Soon, he is Stephanie's father!"

Bandung

Bandung. They had arrived for the night.

They stood in the cool night air, so much fresher than the dry chill inside their bus, waiting for their driver to open the luggage hatch and release their luggage. Their bubbly young tour guide had already gone into the hotel to sort out room placings.

From the first, Annie the tour guide had automatically assigned Stephanie and Steve to a 'double' instead of a 'twin-sharing' room.

"Do you want me to ask her to change it?" Steve had asked Stephanie.

"No," Stephanie said firmly. She had a horror of being noticed as different. She did not want Steve to explain to the pretty tour guide that he and Stephanie were 'only' friends and had to have separate beds even though they were travelling together.

Stephanie had expected that first night in Cerebon to be difficult. After all, it was such a long time since she had shared a bed with anyone. She wasn't even apprehensive about sex. She was apprehensive about being able to relax enough to go to sleep with another body beside hers.

Stephanie had been afraid that Steve might be even more uncomfortable. Could this be the first time this gay man had ever shared a bed with a woman?

To Stephanie's surprise, once in bed they had talked quietly. Steve had rubbed her hands for her, to relieve tension, he said, and they had fallen asleep without embarrassment on either side. It had all felt very natural and very comfortable, lying beside a warm, friendly body. When Stephanie woke with a start in the middle of the night, as she had been doing since Ralph's death, the quiet, steady breathing from the warm, friendly body beside hers lulled her comfortingly back to sleep.

On their second day, Stephanie perked up considerably, looking around her and talking, *talking*! Making conversation had been such an impossibility for so long that Stephanie was amazed by how easily it came back to her.

And now she was almost looking forward to their second night in the same bed.

"I feel like I'm a school kid out on some sort of excursion," Stephanie told Steve gaily. "Get on the bus, get off the bus, look at this, take a photograph of that, next we 're going to look at this, so please read up all about it first in your books ... "

"Yes, isn't it wonderful?" said Steve.

"A holiday from responsibility. I think that school days are wasted on school children; When I was in school, all I could think of was what I was going to do when I got out of school."

"What did you want to do?"

"Be a vet, of course."

"Why 'of course'?"

"Don't all children want to grow up to be vets?"

"Well ... I didn't."

"And yet you ended up as one? How come?"

"I wanted to be a doctor for a long time. Because my father died of a heart attack on his way to the hospital and he might have made it if he had got there sooner. Then my GP teacher in ACJC pointed out that if that was the case, I should set my goals on being an ambulance driver and not a doctor ... which I suppose made sense in a way. But by then, I realised that I *liked* dealing with living systems, you know, figuring out how they work? How you can get them working again? I applied for Medicine, but it was bad timing. That was the year that they first put a quota on the number of 4A students who could do Medicine. I spent three months cleaning bedpans and walking around Woodbridge as an orderly, but the board decided I didn't have the right vocation for the profession ... in a way, I'm glad things turned out this way. I'm glad I'm not dealing with human patients."

"Why?"

Steve laughed, "I hear about the problems some of my ex-classmates are having. The Singapore Medical Association recommends 10 dollars a consultation, but if you have a clinic in an HDB estate, your patients try to bargain you down to eight dollars, inclusive of medicine! People do comparison shopping. And when you do get patients, you spend your days dispensing Panadol, Panadol, Panadol. If you try to get someone to go to see a specialist, they think you're palming them off and move on to another GP; but since news of what happened to the two BGs came out, everyone wants to be referred to a specialist if they get a pimple in the wrong place! And besides, animals don't tell you what they think is wrong with them, and what they think that you should be doing. People talk a bit too much."

"Sorry, tell me if I'm talking too much!"

Steve laughed, "You could never talk too much. I mean, you could never talk so much that I wouldn't want to listen to you."

Steve looked serious as he said this. Stephanie liked the way Steve made the most flippant of remarks with a straight face.

The other people on the bus took for granted that Steve and Stephanie were married; or perhaps they just took for granted that Steve and Stephanie were a couple and kindly decided to accept them as married.

Did it really make a difference?

Travelling with Steve, Stephanie felt as though she had been given all the best parts of marriage with none of the drawbacks. Steve was so attuned to Stephanie that without a word from her, he could detect a broody thought passing through her mind. For instance, in the afternoon when she was looking out of the bus window, believing that he was asleep.

"Stephanie? Is something bothering you?"

"No, I was just thinking about something that I read in the newspapers just before we left Singapore."

"War? Famine? Religious riots? Ecological disaster? Retro-70s fashion?"

Stephanie wasn't a hundred percent sure that Steve wasn't teasing her.

"I read about a woman, this housewife, who killed three of her children."

"I saw that," said Steve. "Terrible."

"At first, I just thought, yes it's so terrible. She must have been a mad woman. But then we don't know anything about what her life was like ... how could a woman get up and do something so completely irrational and destructive like that? I mean, what could she have been thinking? And then I thought, some man must have done something so terrible to her, that she ended up doing something terrible like this. But then her husband sounded so nice, so that wasn't it either. I mean, there were times when I thought, I can easily go mad. I'll just stop trying to behave rationally and let go and I won't be responsible for myself any more. I'll be mad. That woman did that, didn't she? She just let go. It scares me because that could so easily have been me. Or maybe I've already gone mad, and I just don't know it."

Stephanie had been afraid that Steve would laugh at her, but Steve didn't laugh.

"Stephanie, you're not mad."

"How would you know? You don't have any idea of what I think, or of who I really am!"

Stephanie raised her voice and some of the people on the bus turned to look at them in surprise. Steve smiled at them reassuringly before turning back to Stephanie. Steve's voice was always low and moderated. It was a voice designed not to alarm a frightened or hurt animal.

"No. But you don't know everything about yourself either. You're under stress. Don't be so quick to judge yourself when you're already under stress."

"But what else *can* I do?"

"Accept the fact that you feel terrible about yourself. Accept the fact that right now you don't know what to think, that you don't know what to do, that you're unhappy … you don't have to try to control everything. You don't have to control the way other people see you or think about you or how you feel about yourself. You don't have to know how you're going to live the rest of your life. You only have to decide what you're going to do with this moment, then with the next moment, and the next … as they come. Tonight you may decide that you want to spend the next two years in Indonesia, but at any moment in those two years it's up to you to decide whether you want to go through with it or whether you want to change your mind. And if you change your mind, don't see it as a failure of will. As you see more of life, you see life differently. You set different goals. Different things become important to you. You change. Once you know that, it becomes one of the wonders and the glories of being alive!"

The old man dozing.

The dog limping down the road.

Their fellow tourists.

The cool night air.

Stephanie suddenly felt flushed through with a love for all her fellow beings in their collective yet individual journeys through life. Joy and release surging through her made her want to laugh aloud.

"Where did you learn so much wisdom?" Stephanie asked, gently teasing, touched by awe and affection.

"Oh, from animals … " said Steve. For the first time, Stephanie saw him look embarrassed, " … from a mother who sometimes talks too much and analyzes way too much but has a good heart anyway … "

"Why did you ask me to come on this trip with you, Steve?" Stephanie asked.

"Because I fell in love with you the first time I saw you," she thought she heard him say. "Annie's beckoning to us. We'd better hurry!"

But she wasn't sure.

The next morning the tour brought them to Ciater.

Annie the guide had told them a lot about Ciater, but all that Stephanie remembered was that the hot water came from underground springs in Tangkuban Perahu, which they would visit the next day. They had been to so many different scenic tourist spots in the past few days that Stephanie hardly registered the words that filled the bus for their edification.

All she registered was how comfortable she was with Steve and how much she was going to miss him once this tour was over.

The hot springs at Ciater proved to be the beginning of Stephanie's new beginnings. The steam rose richly and voluptuously out of water that ran gaily and purposefully over the rocky stream bed.

While their fellow bus mates were still standing around and posing for photographs, Steve took off his shoes and socks purposefully. Then he rolled up his trousers.

All this he did so naturally that Stephanie followed suit without realising that had Steve asked her if she wanted to paddle, she would have refused out of embarrassment and probably have gone back to sit in the bus.

Then Steve went carefully into the water, dipping first one foot then the other, gingerly, till he could submerge both feet and stand in the gently steaming water, immersed up to mid-calf. He held out his hand to Stephanie.

At first touch, the water was scalding hot on her feet but she hardly noticed.

It was days since she had touched up the polish on her toe nails. It was years since she had held a man's hand. Startled, Stephanie drew back instinctively. From the hot water and from Steve. But when Steve laughed, naturally, unaffectedly and boyishly, she found herself laughing too.

"Gently, gently," he said.

The water was hot, but if he could stand it, so could she. And she did.

Soon, Stephanie was standing in the stream beside Steve. She had never felt so daring and adventurous.

She liked the feeling.

The other tourists, from their bus and others, looked at them as though envying their initiative. Stephanie heard a child asking her father if she could paddle in the stream too.

The father hesitated, then said 'no' in Cantonese.

But why? The little girl wanted to know.

Because your feet will get wet, she was told.

Steve stepped in there. He told the father, in his not-flu-ent-but-adequate Cantonese, that he had plenty of paper towels that the girl could dry her feet with. The man melted. That was all right, he said graciously. His wife had also brought paper towels.

Go and paddle in the water, he urged his daughter, *go on, go on, go on, what's there to be scared of? See, the Aunty is in the water already!*

'Aunty' felt wonderful. If it so happened that you weren't the first woman in space, you could at least be the first woman in the hot springs. You could still make a difference to someone.

In their hotel room that night (their second-last night together), Stephanie lay on her back and watched her toes in the air.

"Hot water is so *heavenly,* don't you think? Especially for the *feet.* I feel so totally relaxed now. Soaking feet in hot water is such a luxury. It must be like shiatsu, don't you think so? I don't see why we don't do it more often.'

"A shortage of hot springs in Singapore might be part of the problem?" suggested Steve prosaically. He sat on the edge of the bed, towelling his hair dry after his shower.

"Yes, but still … you can get basins of really hot water, something like that. Just put your feet in. The problem with taking showers is, it may be very hygienic and all, but by the time the water reaches where your feet are, it's already cold. Or cooling, anyway."

Stephanie rolled to the edge of the bed and looked at Steve upside down.

"You're really sweet, you know that? I'm glad I came. You know, it's so sad? To think that the only man I'm really comfortable with is gay? I don't think that I really *like* straight men at all."

"It's a bit unfair to judge all men by one husband," Steve said.

"I'm not."

"There's been more than one husband?"

"Come on, Steve. Don't tease. You know what I mean. You probably know more about men than I do!"

The words that she spoke so flippantly sounded wrong once they hung in the air. Steve, so sweet and accessible a moment ago suddenly felt like an unpredictable stranger.

"What do you mean, Stephanie?"

"Well – I – " Stephanie was tired and close to tears, "I just meant, the only man I was ever with was my husband … "

Steve just looked at her. Steadily. Lovingly.

"I mean – you're gay, aren't you?"

"No. Not right now, I'm not."

Steve cupped Stephanie's face in both his hands and kissed her.

Stephanie thought, with the small detached part of her mind that was still thinking, *the perfect ending to a perfect day.* Stephanie Lake, nee Chen, had found herself a mission in life at last. She was converting a gay man to a life on the straight and narrow. And she wasn't doing too badly for herself, either.

Final Connections

"This Charlotte Goei says that Stephanie is her daughter," Margaret Chen told Jaylin over the phone, "and while I haven't talked to your Uncle Michael yet ... "

"You believe this woman, Mom? Come on!"

"Yes, I think I do. Yes, I do, Jay."

"But earlier on you said that she was half-crazy ... she just walks into your place and starts making these wild accusations ... I think she's crazy!"

"I thought so. I thought so at first, but when she started talking, everything she said made sense. You should have been here. This woman was sitting so primly on my sofa with her hands folded in her lap ... she looked so respectable! She was wearing this flowered cotton frock and sensible shoes ... "

"And Chin Soon recognised her, you said."

Jaylin wasn't sure whether she was fascinated, horrified, shocked or thrilled. Perhaps all of the above. What is a tragedy to those involved becomes a comedy at one remove. And over the telephone in her office on an otherwise normal, sane day, the news was unbelievable.

"Charlotte panicked when she suspected she was pregnant because she wasn't married. She believed that she was in love with Chin Soon, and she says she has never loved anyone else since … but they weren't married and she panicked and she didn't know how to tell him or what to do … Constance and Michael were leaving for England and so she just went with them. It seemed to be the perfect solution for her to go into hospital as Constance, and for Michael and Constance to take her baby as theirs when they came back to Malaysia … no one knew them in England. Everybody took their word for who they were … "

"So this woman is Stephanie's mother, not Aunty Constance … and *Chin Soon* is Stephanie's father?"

"Apparently," said her mother's voice over the phone drily.

"Don't quite know what he saw in her. She was going on and on about how she's always tried to be around to watch out for Stephanie, I get the feeling she isn't quite all there, if you know what I mean."

"She probably wasn't like that before. All those years of hanging around and watching out for Stephanie probably drove her crazy. I think it's very easy to go crazy watching Stephanie."

"Crazy is not a nice word, Jay."

"You know something, Mum? This means that Stephanie is not really my cousin … that means we can wash our hands of her."

"Jay! She's been your cousin for over 30 years! Just because you find out that she isn't related to you doesn't suddenly make her not your cousin!"

"By the way, what does Chin Soon have to say about all this? I mean, it does rather concern him too, doesn't it?"

"Him!"

Jaylin heard her mother's familiar laugh over the phone. She couldn't be feeling all that bad, then.

"Chin Soon doesn't know whether he's coming or going. But just think, if you were him … one day your girl friend disappears and tells you that she never wants to see you again. Over the years you get used to the idea … it takes longer for you because you need time to get used to things … and then you meet someone else … and lo and behold, the new woman in your life turns out to be the supposed aunt of a girl who turns out to be *your* daughter by the *first* woman in your life who you thought you would never see again … "

"So how is he taking it?"

"You know the man. It will take about a week for it to really sink in. Maybe another week for him to react … and then if at that point in time, he finds he can't handle it, he can always walk away … "

"But are *you* all right, Mother?"

"I don't remember the last time I had so much excitement. I could get used to this!"

"If it's true, it was pretty awful of them never to have told Stephanie."

"They were trying to protect her."

"Then why tell now?"

"Charlotte's idea was to prevent her from making the same mistake her mother had made."

"It's so incredible. It's so mad. No one ever suspected?"

"Who thinks of suspecting something like that? Your Uncle Michael is a very good man, you know. I think that as far as he is concerned, Stephanie is his child."

"I guess in a way she was. And she still is, you know, Mum. I gather *she* still doesn't know about all this?"

"Stephanie was such a sweet child, such a beautiful child. She was such a joy to us all. The first grandchild, you know. Constance was always so protective about her, but then that was just Constance's style, you know ... "

"No one's told Stephanie yet, right? This is going to be some shock for her! The things parents do to their kids!"

But at this her mother fell silent.

"Mum?"

'I'm sorry, Jaylin. I know your father and I haven't been the best of parents."

"Puh-leese, Mum, you've done fine."

"I tried, you know. I was always afraid that one day you would turn around and ask me why I drove your father away."

"Look, Mum, do you know that for years I believed that Dad left because of me?"

"Because of you?"

"Because I told him to go and he left. You didn't know that, did you, Mum?"

"Jay, what happened with your father had nothing to do with you – but I've always worried whether it was because of all that that you turned out ... you know ... "

"Mum – "

" ... whether what happened between your father and me had something to do with how you can't relate to men. I've always felt bad about that, but I never knew what to say to you – and you know I liked Gerry very much ... I never understood why she left you like that ... I just want you to be happy, you know, Jay."

"Thanks. But you know, Mum, I relate to men just fine ... some of my best friends are men. I just happen to find it more natural to love women, that's all. Look, Gerry came from a perfectly happy family ... her parents have a wonderful marriage, and yet she – well, we were in love. I know she loved me. And I loved her. I don't understand why she left either. At that time, I don't think that even she did. She just had to, that's all."

'I'm sorry, Jaylin."

"Nothing to be sorry about, Mum. But Mum ... "

"Yes?"

"Why did Charlotte leave Chin Soon even though they both loved each other – why didn't they just get married? Chin Soon would have married her, wouldn't he? Why didn't she just tell him?"

"Who knows?"

That's My Baby

"No," said Michael Chen, "Stephanie is my daughter. Stephanie has always been my daughter, Stephanie will always be my daughter. That's all there is to be said on the matter. And none of you are going to say anything to her, either. Case closed.

"Charlotte, you mention this to *my* daughter and you are going to find yourself in a mental asylum for the rest of your life.

"Is this clear with everybody?

"Good."

Tangkuban Perahu

"Yes, it was your fault," Steve Thurairatnam said.

Stephanie looked at him, surprise making her mouth hang open. Everyone else who had said anything to her on the subject had assured her that Ralph's death was not her fault at all. She was surprised and a little indignant that Steve agreed so easily that it had been her fault. *But it wasn't*, she wanted to say, contradicting what she had just told him.

"You don't know how it happened," she said, instead.

"I have a good idea of what happened."

"What, then?"

"Your husband fell by accident, your husband killed himself, I know that. But you still say that it's your fault."

"I can't stop feeling that I'm responsible – "

"For what?"

"For his dying. For the way he died."

"No. He was responsible. You're feeling guilty because you ignored him as a person, because you didn't give him the consideration that he deserved as a human being. You could only see him as the husband you didn't love any more. So when he died he wasn't a person for you. That's what you're guilty of – of seeing him as less than a human being … "

"I know," said Stephanie.

"Once you know that you are guilty you can forgive yourself," said Steve.

"There's so much … "

Steve took out his little blue notebook. He folded it back on itself and handed it to Stephanie.

"Write it all down," he said, " – everything. Don't worry, I won't read it."

Stephanie wrote down all that she felt about Ralph Lake's death.

Then she wrote down all that she remembered of her life with him.

Then she wrote down all that she felt about him.

Then she wrote down all she could remember of what she had once felt for him.

Stephanie wrote down the confused heart-deep feelings she had for her late husband. She wrote them all down in Steve's blue-lined notebook, sitting on flat stones on top of the slope that slid, beyond the rails, down into the crater of the volcano.

All around, people were walking, talking, taking photographs, and looking about with curiosity. Vendors were selling souvenirs and jagong.

Serenely, Steve sat beside her. When Stephanie glanced across to him, he caught her movement and turned to smile at her. Stephanie realised that Steve was no more out of place at the rim of a crater of a live volcano than he was in a veterinary surgery in Singapore.

Stephanie herself felt like an outsider everywhere she went. But now she was with Steve, and his in-placeness rubbed off on her and made her feel comfortably belonging, too.

Finally, Stephanie could think of nothing more to write down.

"Done?"

"Yes."

Steve held out his hand for the notebook. Trusting him, Stephanie handed it over.

Then, as Stephanie watched, Steve's strong hands tore out the pages she had written on. Without reading her writing, he folded the pages lengthwise, again and again, till he had a compact tube in his hands.

Stephanie felt that she was watching him perform some ancient and complicated ritual. It was a game and yet it was the one game that it was necessary for them to play in this place and at this time, and she knew that this ritual was the only reason they had come together to this place.

The compressed roll of paper went into the mouth of the empty plastic Fanta Orange bottle. The cap of the Fanta Orange bottle was screwed back on. Inside, the wad of paper unfurled and blossomed to fill space in the bottle.

Then Steve took the bottle to the railing and, as the wind whipped Stephanie's hair across her face, she watched him fling the bottle up and out into the crater in a wide arc.

It spun as it flew up, then fell, bottom first. It bounced against the side of the crater and flew outwards and downwards again.

Stephanie's attention flickered away for an instant wondering if any of the people milling around them had seen what Steve had done. No one seemed to have noticed.

When she looked back, she could not tell where the bottle had gone. For a moment she was afraid as though knowing where the bottle lay would preserve something that was now lost to her forever. Then she realised that she hadn't lost anything she didn't want to lose. She was glad to be rid of it.

"Remember," said Steve, "any time you remember something or feel bad about something that you can't handle, tell yourself you already wrote it down, you already wrote it down and got rid of it and it's buried inside the volcano forever."

Stephanie was free, as though she had offered her soul up for absolution and it had just been returned to her clean, fluffy and scented with freedom.

"You know something?"

"Tell me."

"He wasn't really such a bad guy – Ralph, I mean."

Steve smiled at her, listening. Suddenly it seemed very important to Stephanie that she had to convince him of this.

"He wasn't really. And I loved him, once. I just stopped, somewhere along the way. It was my fault. I stopped being m love with him and he didn't know what he'd done wrong … and it wasn't even his fault. I wasn't interested in him any more. I didn't like him any more. It was all me … "

"No," said Steve, "it was both of you. But it's over. Let it go. It's time to go on."

It is true that time changes your perspective on things. A year ago, Stephanie would not have believed it if someone had told her that she would find salvation in a volcanic crater with a plastic soft drink bottle.

"Ralph told me that you were gay … for a while I even thought that maybe you and him … "

"What do you think now?"

"I think … "

Stephanie couldn't finish her sentence.

"You know, of course, that I love you, Stephanie.

"I love you too, Steve."

Steve took Stephanie's hand and squeezed it shyly.

Their eyes did not lock together in instant and eternal understanding.

They did not kiss passionately and voraciously.

They did not tumble into the scraggy grass on the slopes of the volcano to tear off their clothes and merge bodily warmth and bodily fluids.

Instead Steve smiled at Stephanie.

Stephanie smiled back.

"You know something, Steve. I've just realised I love you. But I think I still *like* you more than I love you."

"I like you too. I like you more than I adore you, which is saying a lot. You know what this means, don't you?"

"Tell me."

"This means that we'll always be friends. We may fall in love, we may fall out of love, but we'll always be friends ... "

Stephanie laughed.

"Even after we're married," said Steve, "we'll be friends."

"Are you asking me to marry you?"

"No."

"No?"

"No. I'm going to court you. Flowers, presents, singing telegrams, good movies, bad poetry ... then I'll come with a ring and go down on my knees and ask you to marry me. How does that sound?"

"Where have you been all my life?"

They walked down the slope hand in hand. Slowly, because of the loose stones. Their fellow tourists were still on the slopes and the bus was empty.

They were besieged by vendors offering food, souvenirs, sweets and postcards.

Stephanie no longer found them oppressive. They were full of life, full of their drive to make a living. Their demands were part of the game of their lives. She had been making too much of the game of her life. She would learn to play; but she would play like Steve, with honour, with dignity and with humour.

Steve bought a wooden humming top. He also bought them charcoal-roasted jagong. The cobs were hot to their hands as they peeled back the moist leaves. The nestled kernels were plump and shiny in their orderly rows. Without salt, without butter, the fresh vegetableness of their being was ambrosial.

From that day on, the taste of jagong was the taste of happiness for Stephanie.

7:35 P.M.

After she put down the phone, Jaylin found it difficult to turn her mind back to her work. She couldn't focus on anything that she had to do. Even the urge to telephone Dr. Lim SuFern (yes, she admitted that) which she had felt so strongly in the past few days had subsided Instead, she found herself opening her briefcase and taking out the unopened letters that she had carried around with her for so long.

Jaylin couldn't say why she hadn't read any of Gerry's letters. It was true that there was no point at all in hanging onto the past, especially when the past had already walked away from you so decisively. But then why had she been carrying all those unopened letters around with her all this time?

Almost without thinking, Jaylin's hands sliced open a pale blue envelope along its seam and a card fell out with Gerry's familiar writing:

You can't stop now
You don't understand
You've been running since you were born

We've come a long way
We've a long way to go
We're all mice in the mouse marathon

Jaylin smiled at the drawing of a cartoon mouse on a treadmill. Gerry had always been good with a pencil. She unfolded the letter tucked inside the card. One thing she had to give Gerry credit for: Gerry had never stopped writing in the face of Jaylin's silence.

I've realised a great many things since getting here. Among them that … the mouse marathon goes on for you not because you expect to get somewhere, but because – because as long as you can still run, the wheel keeps spinning beneath your feet and there is assurance in knowing that you are a part of the world and the world is still alive.

The earth is turning beneath my feet too. I don't know if we'll ever be together again but I know I love you and I want you to know that too. Whatever you want, I want for you. GO FOR IT! *If anybody can, you can. You'll always be my superstar.*

Jaylin found that she was smiling as she folded the note back into its envelope. As far as she was concerned, everybody should have a shot at living happily ever after. And 'everybody' including Lee Jaylin. Lee Jaylin was going to see to that personally.

Jaylin leaned back in her ergonomic office chair and slid out a can of Pepsi. Her phone buzzed.

"Jaylin?" said Mun Ee on the intercom.

"Yes?"

"Raffles Multiplex. Line One."

"Thanks, Mun Ee. And Mun Ee?"

"Yes, Jaylin?"

"Thank you."

"Thank you?"

"For being such a great back up. And for never forgetting to stock up my fridge!"

"Oh, oh, you're welcome, you're very welcome!" flustered Mun Ee.

Jaylin eased up the pull-tab and drank. The good, familiar shock of cold effervescence hit her like a charge of energy.

It was good to be back.

It was good to go on. When she was good and ready, she picked up her phone.

"Yes, Maria?"

"They loved it!" Maria's voice was a pitch above her normal. "They really, really loved it! All out, hundred percent. You did it, Jaylin! They can't wait for the details . . After setting up here they want to set up in Australia, in Canada and in Japan … Golden Age Hotels, Golden Age Tours … this is going to be *so* big, Jay! We've got to talk, when can we meet?"

Opening her Filofax, Jaylin slipped Gerry's card in as a marker.

You can't stop now
You don't understand
You've been running since you were born

You've come a long way
There's a long way more
It's one hell of a mouse marathon

She would write to Gerry. She would finally get around to writing to Gerry.

I've done some thinking of my own.
It's not winning the race that matters.
It's not even whether you finish or not.
It's the dignity with which you run.